The Wild Cats of Piran

Chronicle One

The Wild Cats of Piran

Chronicle One

Scott Alexander Young

Illustrated by Moreno Chistè

Young Europe Books

Published by New Europe Books, 2014
Williamstown, Massachusetts
www.NewEuropeBooks.com

ISBN: 978-0-9900043-0-1

Cataloging-in-Publication Data is available from the
Library of Congress.

Printed in China

First U.S. edition

10 9 8 7 6 5 4 3 2 1

CONTENTS

CHAPTER 1   Queen in the Moonlight................   1

CHAPTER 2   Eight Lives and Counting   15

CHAPTER 3   Kitty-Napped   29

CHAPTER 4   Something Fishy at Lunch..........   41

CHAPTER 5   Night Visions   54

CHAPTER 6   The Lady in Waiting.....................   67

CHAPTER 7   The Battle of Cape Madonna   80

CHAPTER 8   Like Herding Cats   93

CHAPTER 9   The Merchant of Venice   106

POSTSCRIPT   119

. . . And so life goes on, inside my hideyhole in the crypt, some nights with my hidden microfilm camera and ultrasound recording device observing the cat colony in its natural habitat. (Along the way, I've become quite fluent in Cat.) On other nights I sleep under the stars in the nature preserve that is just a short walk or sail from Portorose. Yet I've not become entirely animal-feline. Some time before my money ran out I rather sensibly bought an old wooden fishing boat and learned to catch fish by trial and (much) error. You'd be very proud of me in that respect, living the natural life. Getting in and out of the crypt takes some doing, but one day I broke down and told one of the monks of the Saint George Basilica my entire story. Instead of calling for men in white coats to take me away to a mental asylum, he was really very understanding. We've become sort of friends, I suppose; he's the only other human person (aside from you) I can talk to about any of this.

—letter to Niki Gudmansdottir,
postdate Piran, from a later chronicle

THE WILD CATS OF PIRAN ARE A COLONY of smart, courageous, if also rather lazy feral cats that live in a small seaside town on the Adriatic Sea. Indeed, Piran is a kind of miniature "Slovenian Venice": a serene, forgotten place—at least in the eyes of most humans. Every day, the wild cats work the tables of the restaurants along the seafront promenade, hunting for scraps. And the pickings are rich. There's one nasty, cat-hating maître d' to contend with, but the wild cats toy with him. Life is good in Piran.

In the animal realm, and in the sphere of the supernatural, things are rather different. No one knows that better than Felicia, Queen of the wild cat colony. In the summer in which our story begins, she is presented with a perfect storm of troubles, for there are strange forces at work in this genteel town. For one thing, Piran's rats have become mysteriously evolved lately, and are mobilizing under their leader, the sinister "General Rat." As well as the newly formed rat army, there is a German Shepherd and, worse, there are meddling and incompetent humans to deal with.

Can Felicia hold her clan together, against all odds, or is its idyllic way of life doomed to extinction?

The answers, some of them, anyway, are in this first set of nine tales that is bound to please literary cat lovers of all ages.

Though set in the present day, these adventures are written with such a nostalgic tone that one can imagine readers both young and old enjoying them over long afternoons in a snug armchair.

With special thanks to Franz Sidney

1

Queen in the Moonlight

---

*Introducing two of the most important
personages of the wild cats of Piran—
and two of their greatest adversaries.*

It was an absolutely still night in a little seaside place called Piran, sometime in the recent past, the present day, the near future, or just before.

A cat with a midnight-blue coat, as smooth as a silk top hat, tipped along the highest point of the old city walls. This cat's name was Felicia, and she was perhaps the boldest and doubtless the most dashing of a legendary band of feline fatales they call "the wild cats of Piran." These walls were the highest possible vantage point in all of Piran, unless of course you were a bird. Felicia pulled herself up to her full height to survey the little town, which was made up of old stone houses with whitewashed walls and terracotta roofs, a few medieval churches, and a couple of little piazzas and one main one.

It was a serene, picture-perfect place surrounded by cypress-and-olive-tree-covered hills, facing out over the Adriatic Sea. More and more, to the cat named Felicia, the old town of Piran had become everything to her; every place she had ever been or would ever go. As time went by, Felicia found it harder to remember much from her childhood and early lives in Naples. Just occasionally a memory would flicker through her mind of the delicious odors of the fish markets on a summer's day. Or she would recall the Neapolitan slang words her childhood friends had taught her, and her eyes would turn a different shade.

In this world where appearances are so terribly over-important, Felicia was rather a surprising sort of stray cat. After all, she was so elegant and graceful. She was an Oriental Shorthair cat, with a deep and intense gaze that could take your breath away, and eyes, they said, that "sparkled like dewdrops on a lotus leaf." Sitting up straight as she was now, she looked like an Egyptian statue, an immortal. As well as great beauty and charisma, she had extraordinary powers of hearing, sight, and scent. She could sometimes be a bit of a show-off about all this, but who could really blame her? One could easily imagine any number of humans wanting to adopt Felicia, to pet her and proudly have her sit on their laps, kneading her claws into their skirts or trousers. But Felicia had tried living with humans more than once before. As she put it:

"That relationship was not always successful—especially for them."

This night in Piran, from her favorite spot on the old city walls, Felicia tilted her precious little face in the direction of the moon. She summoned all the wisdom of her former lives and all the strength of her ancestors. She gave thanks to the stars for the joyous feeling of freedom in Piran and for the summer that was on its way. Standing up as high as she could, Felicia fixed her gaze on the moon above. Never taking her eyes off of Earth's lonely satellite, she began to chant.

"Gaze at the winged lion," she sang of herself—a lion indeed, with her slight frame and her tiny, delicate-looking paws!

"Gaze at the winged lion that grasps territories, seas, and stars!"

She would have gone on. But she was rudely interrupted.

"Grasps at territories and stars!? Grasps at fish and mice and beetles and the grass on the ground, more like it!"

Another cat's voice from below had interrupted her happiness.

"And what was that, my dear? Winged lion? Ha-ha!"

Felicia, not the least bit surprised, looked down to find Dragan, lolling on the grass and massaging an itchy back as he did so.

"Dragan, what an unpleasant surprise!"

She was only partly serious, for Dragan was Felicia's right-hand-cat, the fighting feline she could always depend upon. A tubby gray Chartreux cat, Dragan was large and muscular, with short fine-boned limbs, big paws, and very fast reflexes. He was frequently admired for his blue-gray and water-resistant, short double coat. Due to the shape of his head, together with the long, tapered muzzle typical of a Chartreux, Dragan often appeared to be smiling. But there was nothing comforting about his devilish Chartreux cat grin. It was the sort of smile you might expect to see on the face of an anarchist bomb maker who enjoys his work.

"A winged lion! Now that is a vision, to be sure," he said, scratching above his eye with the shin of his paw.

"*Silenzio!*" said Felicia.

"I barely said a thing."

"Shhh!"

A raw feline instinct took hold of Felicia. With her sixth sense, she all of a sudden had the feeling that they were being watched. Once again she rose up to her full height, also screwing up her face, so that her lips curled back and her teeth were exposed.

If you'd like the scientific explanation, this is a process called *Flehmening*. It is something every cat does—not only the wild cats of Piran. With their mouths wide open, more chemical aromas are able to pass into what is called a cat's "auxiliary olfactory sense organ." Goodness! That sounds complicated. Well, really it's just something inside Felicia and in every other cat's body that enables them to detect *trouble*, and that's just what Felicia was sure she could smell. Trouble!

It was, in fact, the overpowering stench of a hulking, pubescent lad, and now here he was, running toward them both. He had a neck like a tree trunk and fists the size of grapefruits, a large-size rock in his throwing hand. And he was coming right at them, rock first!

"Dragan!"

"What?"

"*Meooove!*"

Dragan knew enough to know that a "meooove" from Felicia meant business. He shot sideways as fast as he could to dodge the rock being thrown at him with tremendous force by this kid with big hands. Felicia, with her acute sense of split-second timing, could see that it was not going to be fast enough. The rock was speeding toward a head-on collision with Dragan's noble, if grumpy, head. And then it would all be over for him, for as far as she could remember, Dragan was now living his ninth and final life.

There was only one thing to do. Felicia cried out a *Meeeeeeeeooooow*, and the world turned upside down.

The rock the lad had thrown stopped in mid-air, hovering there for a moment or two. Then, as if giving up on the idea of floating, it dropped to the ground. It seemed to take its time doing so—as if someone or something had rewritten the laws of gravity for about half a minute, which is either a long or short time depending on how you think about it. In any case, the boy was vaguely aware that he had witnessed something unusual. But he was not the sort given to speculation about such matters. He was angry, plain and simple. He'd been cheated of a victory. Why, he'd almost dealt that fat cat a mortal blow, something he would've referred to as a "result."

Instead, he'd been outfoxed by a cat! Well, actually by *Majikat*: the use of magic to alter events. Something more than just Felicia using her supernatural superfeline strengths to disappear in a flash; or, for that matter, to pull the shoelaces from the boy's sneakers. Incidentally, when it came to Majikat, the wild cats of Piran didn't need to waste a lot of time with hocus-pocus or mumbo jumbo or abracadabras. A single, distinct sounding *Meeeeeeeeooooowwww* in the right frequency would do the trick. It also meant that the wild cats would have to ration their use of Majikat until the next New Moon—but more about that in due course.

Dragan went to pick himself up, but in an instant, the teenage boy had leapt on top of the tubby Chartreux, putting all the weight of his body into it. Dragan squirmed and clawed and bit for all he was worth. But the boy was strong, even stronger than he looked. Felicia had slid down the wall and was now hiding in the shadows, where she had found the rock the boy had thrown at Dragan. Without a second's more hesitation, she picked up the rock and threw it at the cruel adolescent.

"Owwwwww!" It bounced off his forehead with a *boing*, which is not how rocks usually behave. Then again, Majikat had a way of affecting everything it touched.

The nasty, cat-taunting teenager fell to one side, giving Dragan just enough time to get up and make a run for it. Although the plump cat may have looked "generously proportioned," Dragan could be a fast mover. But the young brute of a human had soon scrambled back to his feet. His face was crimson with rage.

"If only Thor were here," he said. This was something that didn't make much sense to Felicia or Dragan at the time. He looked around him wildly, trying to find the cats' eyes shining in the darkness. Dragan had run to Felicia's side, and they stood huddled together in the shadow of the city wall. They dared not move or make a sound.

"Come on, you little pussycats. I'm not going anywhere until I find you."

The wild cats of Piran are constantly being underestimated. And this would be one of those occasions. No adolescent boy, bristling with superfluous energy, could match a cat for patience.

And so he waited.

And the wild cats waited.

And he waited a little more.

Finally, after around forty-five minutes, the boy gave up. Felicia and Dragan stayed perfectly still until they were sure he was a safe distance away. Then, silent as a tear falling from a statue, the two wild cats of Piran disappeared softly into the night.

YOU WILL FIND THE CHARMINGLY SLEEPY TOWN OF PIRAN on the coastline of Istria, which is possibly a place you have never heard of, so don't pretend if indeed you haven't. That's really perfectly all right. Istria is the largest peninsula on the Adriatic Sea—which, as has been established, is the body of water Piran looks out over. And Piran is, more precisely, on that part of the peninsula that lies within Slovenia, another place you might not be very familiar with. Slovenia is a small and not unhappy European country that shares borders with other countries whose names are Croatia, Austria, Hungary, and Italy.

It is hard to believe, but the greater metropolitan area of Piran contains some 4,000 human beings. It's therefore probably not surprising that out of those thousands, there should've been one really nasty piece of work. We won't name-and-shame this fourteen-year-old oaf by giving you his real appellation and exact address. It's enough to say that "Fisko"—as we shall call him—was very large for his age indeed. His parents, who were away most of the time, gave Fisko far too much money to spend on stupid activities and possessions. Fisko was old enough to have grown out of pulling the wings off flies, but he hadn't. Grown out of it, that is. The larger the animal, so long as he could dominate it or cause it pain, then the better, as far as this rather nasty piece of work was concerned.

This destructive, pubescent monster was nothing but bad news as far as the wild cats of Piran were concerned. When they were both sure they were safely hidden, Felicia and Dragan watched the hulking teenager traipse slowly back to a quite large villa on the hills over the town, kicking a can as he went.

"He is larger than others like him, *e anche più brutto* (and uglier than most)," whispered Felicia in the Human Italian language to Dragan.

"No argument there, Queenie. Listen, I'm sorry about that, fooling around . . . you *are* a winged lion, truly you are, Felicia."

"It's alright, Dragan. You don't have to thank me for saving your life." Dragan squirmed, a little embarrassed. A light went on briefly inside the villa when the boy stepped inside. A dog also started barking somewhere near or inside the house, but then stopped as abruptly as it had started. The old villa into which Fisko disappeared had been sitting vacant for some time, and the wild cats of Piran had played inside it once or twice, making a mess in the fireplace.

"Now this monster moves in," said Dragan. "*Dobry!*" (That is, "Great!" in the Human Slovene language.)

As it would turn out, the boy Fisko, though not the least of the wild cats' problems, was not perhaps their greatest threat to peace and happiness; for while Felicia and Dragan made their way home, a single, beady little eye was watching them from several hundred meters away. And this particular eye belonged to a repugnant example of an especially unpleasant species. The animal in question was nearly half a meter in length. He must have weighed eight kilograms—seventeen pounds, that is—making him enormous for this type of creature. His whiskers twitched, and he creased up his shiny fat snout to smell the early morning sea-breeze.

Now this rat, for a rat it was, had no name. Rats do not really believe in names, but he did have a rank, and was known by all who followed him simply as "General Rat." And every single rat in Piran did follow him. (Well, all except for one who lived with a thirteen-year-old teenage girl who happened to be a self-professed "Goth" and kept her rat—who showed no interest in local politics—as a pet.) The General was a rat who by ratlike standards was a strategic, tactical, military, and political genius. This was because his IQ exceeded fourteen and he could plan ahead more than sixty seconds at a time. This was an enormous leap ahead in rat physiology, and not to be sneezed at, because, potentially, an extra percentage or two of anything that combustible could be the tipping point in the cat-and-rat power balance. General Rat was indeed a rat among rats, a rat for all seasons.

If you are sensibly wondering how the General was able to watch the cats from such a distance, it was due to a telescope he had found on the promenade one day early in the spring. Intelligent enough to understand its purpose, the General had worked out a system whereby he could use the telescope to watch the cats' activities at a safe distance. A safe distance meant well out of the cats' range of smell and hearing. One of the General's eyes was covered with a patch; part affectation, this was, for he was not really blind in that eye. He fancied that the patch made him look more handsome and dashing. He was mistaken.

The telescope was held aloft by two particularly obedient rats, whose names, like those of so many other rats, were simply "rat" and "rat." Balancing himself on the back of another obligingly complaisant rat, whose name too was "rat," the General would stare with his one beady little eye through the viewfinder at whatever he wanted to observe at closer quarters. "I love this system of observing the cats at a distance," the General said, to no one in particular, as he watched the two cats amble home.

"I love this system of observing the cats at a distance," of course sounds completely different in the Rat tongue. Just like Cat, the Rat language is seldom spoken in the presence of humans. Unlike Cat, however, which is a beautiful-sounding language, Rat is an *exceptionally* unpleasant tongue. Thus, the observation, "I love this system of observing the cats at a distance," came out as, "*Ypkxnf, Jwbnq, Ctgexi!*"

In any case, one of the rats answered the General's statement with a question completely irrelevant to the matter at hand. This is what Private Rat had the nerve to inquire:

"What are we going to eat?"

"What are we going to eat!?" General Rat shouted back in reply, his voice charged with fury. Private Rat looked back at him meekly, trying to smile.

"I mean, er, *when* are we going to eat?" Did the private really believe this was an improvement? General Rat's one working eye narrowed to a squint.

"I'll tell you when you're going to eat," he said in a quiet voice that was more frightening than if he had yelled. But then, bellowing, he exclaimed:

"Guards! Seize the prisoner!"

The General motioned to two of his most fearsome-looking personal guards.

"Let's not just eat any old thing at any old place. The private deserves the very best in town, and nothing less will do as far as I'm concerned!"

The two guard rats grabbed Private Rat and restrained him. He squealed and squirmed under their weight, frightened by the no-doubt grisly fate that awaited him. The General was quite gifted when it came to administering punishment. The other rats rather enjoyed this sort of thing, too.

"I wonder what's in store for the private," one rat said to another in what he thought was a whisper. They would not have long to find out.

General Rat with his telescope,
watching the cats from afar.

However, you, dear reader, may have to be a shade more patient. Granted, there may be some who prefer a yarn that spins itself undone from the beginning of its thread all the way to the end. But in Piran, in wild cat circles, at any rate, they like to begin their yarns in the middle, make as big a mess as possible, and then find their way to either side. It may be that you have to be a wild cat to understand this. And it may be that you have become one, by the end of these chronicles.

Stranger things had happened, and were about to again.

2

Eight Lives and Counting

More of the wild cats make their entrance
on the stage of Piran, and the history of
Felicia's eight lives is examined.

It was some time after Felicia and Dragan's nasty brush with the brutish boy, possibly even later the same night. As clouds flitted over the face of the moon, two feral felines slid down the slippery slope outside the Basilica of Saint George. Coming to a halt, they drew themselves up in front of a hole in the ground. It was a small, dim spot on a shadowy foothold, a place difficult for a human to identify in the daytime, let alone past midnight.

Felicia and Dragan were outside the little tunnel that was the cats' secret entrance to a crypt: a subterranean burial chamber underneath the old church. This crypt was indeed the principal secret hiding place for the wild cats of Piran, certainly the one they used most often. Felicia and Dragan emerged from the pitch black into its vast cool chamber. Flinging themselves around in the dim light of the tomb were most of the stray cats that made up their little band. The gang of "*Gatti*" (Italian for "cats") made full use of the old tomb's spaciousness, and of course its members had no trouble at all seeing in the half-light. A few of them were resting on top of coffins; some were hanging from window bars or sprawling on the large cool floor. On the walls of the crypt were painted frescoes of saints and holy men and long-forgotten soldiers from centuries-old wars, all watching over the wild cats of Piran.

Without a doubt, the loudest voice among all the wild cats belonged to Magyar. Magyar was a large, reddish-orange tabby cat with great, long, curling whiskers. Like all tabbies, he had a distinctive coat adorned with stripes, dots, and swirling patterns. According to certain cat pedigree snobs, a tabby isn't actually a recognized breed of cat, but you would not have been advised to tell Magyar that, for he might have got upset and given you a good scratch upside the face. Though perfectly placid at some times, he could be quite ferocious at others, and it was always difficult to predict when he would be which. Magyar had an "M" mark on his forehead, which he said stood for his name, but in fact this pattern was common to all tabby cats. As you may know, *magyar* is simply another way of saying "Hungarian" (in which language it is roughly pronounced *mudyar*). In another life, as a human being, old Magyar might indeed have been a Hungarian Hussar, riding in the cavalry and wearing a spiffy uniform. He would have been the very ideal of an officer—until an actual war began.

"It was raining rats and dogs last night," Magyar was saying when Felicia and Dragan came in. Magyar fancied himself to be the comedian of the group too.

"Raining rats and dogs, that's mildly funny," said Dragan, smiling his eerie smile. Seven pairs of cats' eyes, all shining in the darkness, turned to look. By way of greeting, Felicia and Dragan rubbed faces with every cat present, and each returned the compliment. Any observant cat owner can tell you how rubbing faces is the ultimate cat "seal of approval." If a cat rubs your face with its own, caressing its nose against your upper cheek and forehead, it means you have been named an honorary member of that cat's family. (It's an honor the wild cats of Piran bestow only on one human. Her name is Signora Fortuna, and we shall meet her in due course.)

In any case, Magyar welcomed Felicia and Dragan with enthusiasm:

"*Üdvözöljük!* (Welcome!)" he called out in Hungarian. "Cat dragged in, look what!" He laughed again at his own, awkwardly uttered joke, but received a shove from the female cat standing beside him. This was Beyza, the fluffy Turkish Angora whom Magyar adored above all the others.

"We're late because we almost lost a life on the way here. I had to use Majikat to stop it!" said Felicia. That was enough to stop all other conversation. You see, although none of the other wild cats would be so rude as to mention it, it was a well-known fact that both Felicia and Dragan each had only one of their nine lives remaining. Immediately, the guessing game began.

"What happened? Is there a wolf out there we didn't know about?" asked one of the cats. "Or a particularly vicious and well-organized Rat?" queried another, jokingly, knowing little the truth of its jest.

"If you'll all quiet down for a moment, I'll tell you," said Felicia. "Let's say, *'la situazione é gravissima ma non seria'* (the situation is grave but not serious)," she began. The wild cats gathered close to hear all about the attack by the adolescent boy and Felicia's split-second decision to invoke Majikat. This last revelation caused a bit of tut-tutting and meowing and mewling. The wild cats believed that it was dangerous to use Majikat more than three times every lunar cycle. This was because of some old, unwritten rules.

In any event, after sharing the details of their attack and escape, Dragan and Felicia were disconcerted to learn that this monstrous boy had been on the warpath before.

"This time his dog he didn't have?" asked Magyar. When Magyar was nervous or under pressure—

or even just excited—he would speak in this strange back-to-front manner.

All the other cats' eyes turned to the Hungarian cat.

"It's big, typical German Shepherd dog," said Magyar. Then, seeing that he had everyone's attention: "He drools at the mouth a lot. But a bumblebee could outwit him. Thick-skulled, but potentially deadly: I for one didn't like the look of his front incisors." Magyar looked particularly pleased with himself after this summing up. He had managed a complete and rather complicated sentence without once speaking backward. But instead of congratulations:

"Just when were you going to tell us about this, my Hungarian friend?" Dragan said, with more than a tinge of anger in his voice.

"Him yesterday I only saw: meaning you to tell! Sorry am I. You told have should I . . ."

"Hush, Magyar," said Felicia. "We know what we're facing now, that's all that matters."

At the mention of a German Shepherd, a chill had run through the air. They were all pretty fearless felines, but German Shepherds—well, they're another matter altogether.

"We'd *all* better be careful, no matter how many lives we have left. As we know where they live, let's keep a watch on the villa," instructed Felicia. All the cats nodded in silent agreement. Well, all except for Magyar, who took it upon himself to repeat the proscription, again in his irregular, backward-speaking manner:

"Quite right, everyone. On the lookout, watchful; best way to be: all cats house-watching, possible as soon as."

In his worldview, Magyar saw himself as the leader of the colony of feral cats in Piran. This was an opinion of his status none of the other cats shared, and one they rarely allowed him to indulge. It was natural therefore that it was Felicia who rose to the occasion with a magnificent speech that rallied all the cats around, purring oaths of agreement.

"Friends, Piranese, and feral cats:" Felicia began. "It seems that yet another human monster and his brute dog slave walk among us!" There were low murmurings of assent among all the assembled cats.

"But with life and limb in constant danger, will you ever find a feral cat from Piran quaking in his boots, afraid for however many of its lives he or she has left? No, I say to you!"

"Hear, hear!" rumbled and burbled the wild cats of Piran in support of this thesis.

"Look at us. We are, and must remain, as calm as a windless summer's day on the cobalt blue Adriatic Sea. Calm, but vigilant. *Va bene?* (Is that not right?)"

All of the cats there gathered shouted "Hear, hear!" again and the general feeling of electricity went up a notch.

"After all, my friends," she went on, "the wild cats of Piran have faced dogs before, haven't we? Not to mention headwaiters, more than one police officer, and several fishermen, overeager rats, and the occasional predatory bird."

The cats were cheering and jeering and generally making noise by this point.

"Marvelous!"

"Inspired!"

"Rousing!"

They all agreed on this, after such a stirring speech.

So too they concurred that it was good to be a cat, better yet to be a feral cat, and, best of all, to be a wild cat of Piran.

So how was it, then, that Felicia had become the Queen of the wild cats of Piran, even if it was an unofficial title? Whence did she derive her natural authority? To understand that, you would need to understand something of her past.

Felicia was born into the first of her nine lives on a summer's evening in Naples, in the Year of Our Lord 1721. She was the middle kitten of a litter of five. The five kittens were to be brought up as pets in a mansion house, or more accurately, a "palazzo." This magnificent home had been built for a high-ranking officer in the Neapolitan Navy and his family. Something of this sailor's spirit had passed from master to domestic animal—namely, the longing to set sail and go on adventures.

A wandering spirit of adventure was not something conducive to the life planned for Felicia. Although she was a natural aristocrat, sitting around in stuffy, richly furnished drawing rooms listening to chamber music didn't do much for her. She didn't particularly care to be waited on by servant boys dressed in powdered wigs and shoes with gold buckles. This was more the type of life her mother Alessandra had wanted for her, not to mention the human mistress of the household, a bundle of nervous energy whose full name and title was Contessa Felicia Monteleone.

As well as her "given" name, Felicia inherited certain characteristics from the Contessa: her pride, her effortless style, and her ability to get her own way, even when in the wrong. But Felicia's need to roam the world, which she had inherited from the admiral, was that much stronger, and so one fateful night, stray she did.

She waited until the human household was asleep, and then told one of her cat sisters, "I'm just going out for a drink." This was taken to mean she would take a drink of water from the garden fountain. In fact, once outside, Felicia gripped hold of a climbing vine, shimmied up the wall, and disappeared forever into the sultry Naples evening.

Escape was simple, but saying goodbye was hard, or rather, *not* saying goodbye. You see, Felicia knew that if any of her family thought she was leaving, they would surely have tried to stop her. It was an early lesson to the very young cat, still little more than a kitten. . . .

The lesson was that you sometimes had to be cruel to be kind.

*Felicia with the pirate Edward England
(with his parrot Desmond upon his shoulder).*

Felicia had escaped the privilege of her circumstances and everything safe and reliable. At first, her flight from the Captain's palazzo took her no further than across town to the Spanish Quarter, the poorest of all the poor parts of Naples. Here Felicia learned how to fight and how to steal, and she died the first and second of her nine lives. She emerged stronger and wiser each time.

After a few more years exploring everything the feline underworld of Naples had to offer, Felicia was off on a journey that took in much of Italy and Sardinia, but also a life—several lives—spent at sea. "Before the mast," as they used to say.

She sailed with a Spanish Sardinian merchant ship at first, then later, but not much later, with a legendary pirate captain named Edward England, known as being a comparatively humane pirate, for he tried to kill as few captives as possible. What is not so well known was the part Felicia played in stopping Edward England from executing prisoners. She also persuaded him, using all her feline wiles, to desist from using that hideous whip, the so-called "cat o' nine tails," on disobedient sailors. This is just another example of how the influence of cats is so underwritten in the official version of history.

As a ship's cat aboard a pirate ship, Felicia had of course thrown her lot in with a band of terrifying desperadoes. But, happily, she was well-liked by them all. She became particular friends with Captain Edward England's parrot, a very chatty fellow named Desmond. Friendships like this between cat and bird are quite rare. Like Desmond, Felicia slept in her master's cabin, and together they sailed the seven seas. To Jamaica and then Honduras they went, then past Florida to Virginia and New England. From there it was on to West Africa, before sailing the Cape of Good Hope for the isles of Madagascar, and, later, Mauritius. All along the way Felicia dined on a steady diet of mice and rats and fish, and was considered a good luck mascot by captain and crew.

When the *Fancy,* Edward England's fastest ship and the pride of his fleet, weighed anchor, Felicia would go ashore with the men. She liked nothing better than discovering new tastes, sensations, rhythms, and colors.

Then one day out at sea, Felicia thought she could make out the Italian coastline. The mere idea of it pulled at her heartstrings. It was all over with the pirate life, as far as she was concerned. She longed to be among animals and even humans whose ways were akin to hers. So, the next time the *Fancy* pulled ashore, she jumped ship and caught another on its way to Tunisia, whence she sailed first to Constantinople (or Istanbul, as it is known today), and from there to Venice.

The crew of the *Fancy* had been right about Felicia: she had brought them good fortune. However, the luck of the pirates aboard the *Fancy* ran out almost the instant she left. For history does record that Edward England ended his life of crime as a miserable beggar, dressed in rags.

For decades, Felicia wandered up and down all of Italy, from Palermo to Trieste. She was in Venice, that most serene city, when Napoleon's troops marched in one day in June 1797. Afterward there was a brief stint with the world's most famous colony of feral cats. The Coliseum cats of Rome might have seemed like the natural peer group for Felicia, but she had been born to lead, not to follow. The Coliseum cats already had a virtually invincible Queen, whose name was Agrippina. She and Felicia did not get along.

But she simply could not bring herself to return to Naples. The fact was, Felicia still burned with shame whenever she thought of her desertion from the family litter all those years ago. Her memories were sometimes vague, but that particular one remained raw.

Another of life's lessons: while pain seems to have no memory, shame most certainly does.

However, anywhere else in the "old country" would do. It was all "*Bella Italia,*" and surely that was where she belonged, if anywhere.

So strange, then, that Felicia should end up just over the border from Italy in the little Slovenian town of Piran. She had traveled to Piran by stowing away under the back seat of a car—an Alfa Romeo Giulietta convertible to be precise. Well, by then it was the 1980s and Felicia was on to her seventh life. She had been intending to visit Piran for only a day or two. One or two other cats had told her how pretty it was.

Once there, she had roamed about the old town, and took what she wanted from all those outdoor restaurant tables on the waterfront promenade. As greedy as any cat, Felicia strolled about the place until she came across a fellow feline. It was the rather fierce-looking, blue-gray Chartreux we now know as Dragan. At the time she encountered him, he was eating lunch on the terrace of a stout and kindly Italian lady, headfirst into a bowl of fish stew.

"*Ciao micetto* (Hello kitty)," she had said, indicating the bowl. Encountering no resistance, Felicia dived in headfirst as well. But Dragan had been so preoccupied by eating that he hadn't even noticed Felicia. Now he jumped backward, brandished his claws, and hissed. Felicia looked back at the plump but handsome blue-gray Chartreux and simply fluttered her eyelashes. Dragan was no match for that. He in turn smiled his famous, unsettling Chartreux cat grin.

"Well, what is the meaning of this?" he then huffed, trying to sound as grumpy as possible. "Interrupting a tomcat while he's eating?!"

"My name is Felicia. *Piacere di conoscerti* (It's a pleasure to meet you)."

"Well, I mean to say, they call me Dragan. There's plenty here if you'd like to dig in."

"*Sei molto gentile* (You're very kind)."

There is no greater bond for cats than sharing food, which you will agree is a sound proposition all around. Suffice it to say, the two cats had immediately hit it off. Which is to say, they started bickering and sniping at each other from their very first meeting.

To Felicia's utmost surprise, the little Slovenian town had very quickly begun to feel like home. But it was more than that. Here, finally, everything she had ever learned about leadership, from the Navy man of Naples, the pirate Edward England, and from Napoleon himself, Felicia could put into practice. As must be clear by now, Felicia was not a cat you could cage for long. Throughout her long journey from her hometown of Naples all the way to Piran, she had lashed out more than once at those who had tried taming her. Yet those first two or three decades in Piran had been a walk in the park compared to what was in store for her. All of Felicia's cleverness, strength, and intuition would soon be stretched to the limit, as you, perceptive reader, doubtless foresee.

3

Kitty-Napped

*In which the cuddliest member of the colony is taken
from her sweetheart, and a sobering example of
General Rat's idea of justice is evidenced.*

Dawn and the first fingers of sunlight tinged the floodlights over Piazza Tartini. This is the main market square in the center of Piran. That morning, like every other morning, the famous fiddler Tartini's statue, violin in hand, smiled over the piazza with an air of wicked merriment. His ghost, the devilish violin player, was upstairs in an attic on a house on that very piazza, locked in his nightly struggle to beat the Devil. But that's another story, which we shall save for a little later in these chronicles.

As far as we need be concerned, on Piazza Tartini that morning, all was still and quiet. Then, bounding across the square went Magyar and his ladylove, the cuddly white cat named Beyza. Running fast as they could, the two cats disappeared from the scene, and the large public place resumed its stillness, its ever-so-quiet majesty.

The lovestruck feline duo continued racing uphill until, a little breathless, the two of them came to a stop at the corner. Magyar looked at her with hopeless devotion: she was such a special creature. After all, there aren't that many feral—that is to say, wild—Angora cats in this world, but little Beyza, she was one of them. At a formative age (only onto the second her of nine lives) she had been forced to live in the wild. She had been rescued and taught survival skills by none other than Magyar. Beyza was still a lady of leisure at heart, spectacularly lazy and highly adept at pretending to be less intelligent than she really was. In this way she was able to manipulate most humans and plenty of tomcats—especially Magyar—to get whatever she wanted.

They had paused at the spot where the long, winding Rozmanova Lane met with Gorianova Lane. (Yes, aren't they marvelous names?) Beyza leaned against a wall, trying to appear cool and nonchalant, not as if she had just run out of breath.

"You're faster than you look!" she huffed and puffed.

Magyar and Beyza running across Piazza Tartini, moments before Beyza is captured. A study in motion.

"Well, I know who's chasing me," spluttered Magyar.

"You embarrassed me in the crypt, talking so big again!" Beyza scolded him.

"But I thought you liked me to be a manly sort of a cat. You know, a real tom," he said, in a mock-pathetic tone.

"I said I wanted you to be a gentlecat, not a show-off."

Their eyes met, and all of a sudden the reason one of them had been chasing the other was forgotten. This was how it always was with these two. They had been starstruck lovers ever since the orange tabby had laid eyes on the bundle of furry white Turkish delight. That had been a long time ago, on the *puszta*, or the prairies of Hungary. But on this particular evening in Piran, once they'd caught their breath, the two cats cuddled up to each other in a highly affectionate manner. If any of the other cats had been around, they would have pleaded with them to desist. But the love cats' state of slightly sickly happiness was not destined to last for long.

There was the sound of them at first, for as you'll remember, a cat's sense of hearing is the strongest of its five conventional senses.

"Look, we can get two!" somebody was now shouting.

Then there was the smell and sight of them: a dog and its human racing toward them at a clip. This was Fisko, the cruelly infantile boy who had thrown a rock

at Dragan just a few hours earlier. Now he was running toward them yelling orders to his fierce-looking
German Shepherd.

"Come on, Thor! After them!"

"Grrrrrrrrrrrrrrrrrrrrrrrr!" the canine animal
named Thor managed by way of response. Clearly he
was the thinker of the pair. Well, perhaps thinker
is stretching it a bit, but something in his cranium
must have been sending messages that powered the
dog's legs forward, and sent him hurtling toward two
very frightened cats. This was no time for Magyar
and Beyza to discuss strategy. It was no time for he-
roics, either. Running was the only thing for it, so
they both SPLIT—Beyza in one direction, Magyar in
the other.

Magyar was alright; he was too fast and too slippery for either man or beast. His feet, which had raced
across the great prairies of Hungary, the puszta, had
no trouble disappearing around a corner and shimmying up a drainpipe, out of sight. He jumped onto
the rather flimsy ledge of one of the roofs and swung
up on top in a surprising display of athletic grace. He
sat down on the tile roof and breathed a heavy sigh
of relief. Then, in his most philosophical manner, he
began to discourse:

"Doing they are what!? This is Night of Time!?
Disgrace! Sleep—Ever they don't?" Magyar continued
to bellyache backward in his raspy voice: "Agree you
must dear, I mean you must agree. . . . Dear? Beyza?
Are you . . ."

Then suddenly he stopped blithering and a chill ran down the spine of the old battler from Hungary.

"Beyza?" He waited again.

There was no reply. There was no sound at all. There was no Beyza. Poor, besotted, bewildered tabby cat. Magyar knew it in his femur. He knew it before he even had time to stop and pause and bite his paws with sadness and shame for being such a fool. He had left Beyza behind with that boy and that vicious dog! He was a selfish, silly old puss. Hadn't she repeatedly told him so? Why hadn't he listened?

Enough time wasted in useless remorse. Magyar picked himself up and bolted straight back the way he had come. The corner was deserted, but with his acute sense of hearing Magyar began to trace the sound of Beyza's muffled cries. Muffled? What was that? He concentrated as hard as the greatest of Hungary's famous concert pianists. Still following the sounds, he took a right turn back onto Rozmanova Lane.

The truth of it was, Magyar already knew in his brittle cat bones where the sounds were coming from. There was a dull laugh and a low canine growl mixed in with Beyza's sad mewling. Beyza must have been captured by the brutes. No other conclusion was possible. The noises led him to the villa that Felicia had described earlier. Magyar finally drew up close enough to see that Fisko had a small backpack slung over his shoulder, inside of which had been stuffed a Turkish Angora cat: his beautiful, fluffy Beyza.

Magyar considered for a moment jumping up onto the backpack and tearing it open with his claws. That would have meant invoking Majikat to make him even stronger and faster, a real adversary for the German Shepherd. But without Felicia's permission? For all his bravado, Magyar didn't dare risk it. But without Majikat, it was hopeless. There was something intimidating about this boy's swagger. There was definitely something intimidating about the German Shepherd, stopping and sniffing the air as it made its way up the path to their front door. So Magyar held back, and waited in the shadows. The gate and then the door of the villa clicked shut. Magyar's poor old heart sunk into the soles of his paws. Because, oh, how terribly sad he was that he could not "let the cat out of the bag."

Down on the streets below, shuttered windows were being pulled open, and lights were switching on inside houses. The old seaside town of Piran was beginning to yawn and stretch into a state of awakening. This is the saddest time of the day for most feral cats. It is the hour when the world of shadows and play and mystery, the feline world of the night, is replaced with the rather more humdrum and human world of daytime. It was doubly sad for Magyar, who had lost Beyza, his ladylove.

AND WHAT OF DOINGS A RUNG OR TWO LOWER in the food chain? Referring generally to *Rattus Norvegicus*? You haven't forgotten them, now have you? You will recall a certain Private Rat had been sentenced to some sort of dreadful punishment by General Rat. So it was that Private Rat was carried to a back alley behind the waterfront restaurants along the promenade. By this time, the private was blubbering:

"Please, please no: I'll do anything. . . . I'll even . . . take a bath!"

A couple of the other rats shuddered at the very idea. A bath!? Truly, as far as most rats were concerned, that *was* a fate worse than death.

Instead the two guard rats bundled the prisoner into the tiny little courtyard at the rear of a restaurant-cum-tavern named after Martin Kirpan, which we shall henceforth refer to as the Martin Kirpan Tavern. They hid behind the back door to the kitchen, waiting for it open. The instant the door swung open, the two guards heaved the squealing Private Rat in front of it and ran away as fast as they could. Stepping outside at that exact moment was the maître d'. (The term means the master of the restaurant and is French, which this gentleman liked to think he was.)

The maître d's real name was not Gaston, as he invariably told people it was, hoping to affect an air of Gallic sophistication. He was an uncomfortably tall, wiry man with oily hair and luxuriant moustaches brushing his cheeks. He had been on his way outdoors to smoke one of his stinky little cigars. Almost immediately, though, he saw the rat scuttling for cover and swung into action without a moment's hesitation. Not knowing which way to run, Private Rat ran between the maître d's legs and toward the kitchen inside.

"RAAAAAAAAAAAAAAAAAAAT!!!!" screamed the maître d', spinning on his heels and following the hapless private inside. The rat, frightened out of his wits, ran straight toward a corner and tried to hide under a large sink full of dirty cutlery. But this kitchen was that of the maître d', his home turf. He saw exactly where the rat had fled, and he knew just where to find a good, sharp cleaver. Private Rat tried to make a run for it, but the maître d'—Gaston—had him cornered.

"Why, you filthy little vermin!" he shrieked, bringing the cleaver down on the rat's neck, severing his head from his body. We are sorry to distress the sensitive reader with an account of such barbarity, but these are the sad facts of the matter.

As far as General Rat was concerned, his one working eye watching from the safety of his telescope, the execution had gone off splendidly. Rats don't have much of a sense of humor—just the same, they all laughed along obediently when the General rolled back his head and cackled loud and long. What a witty fellow their leader was, as well as being a strategic and tactical genius.

Unsurprisingly, perhaps, Private Rat later became the chief ingredient in a rather good *Ratatouille*. But that's another story, eh, best told by someone else? Anyway, if the rats of Piran would do that sort of thing to each other, imagine what they'd like to do to the wild cats of Piran! On second thought, for now, you'd better not. The fantasy life of a rat isn't anywhere we recommend spending more time than strictly necessary.

IT WAS AROUND MIDDAY WHEN MAGYAR WOKE UP. He had been sleeping for seven hours. Now that might sound like a lot—especially in the midst of a crisis—but for a cat of his shape, proportions, and disposition, it was really no time at all. Stirring in his shaded nook under a tree, he stretched and yawned and generally untangled himself. It took him a moment or two to register Beyza's absence. His whole nature and force of habit were so attuned to her being present. To say he feared the worst is to put it mildly. That brute of a boy and that savage dog, what terrible plans had they in store for his beloved? Just as he was pondering this, Felicia and Dragan came ambling up the path toward him.

"You look a bit off-color, Magyar. Not your usual orange self?" This was Felicia.

"Upset a little I look! Too be would you! Kitty-napped was Beyza night last!"

"Oh, Magyar," said Dragan. "You poor, daft old tabby!" This was about as sensitive and consoling as Dragan ever got. Sentimentality was not really his style.

All at once, there was a noise from the villa that gave everyone pause. It was the sound of the front door opening. To avoid being seen, or sensed, the three cats crouched even lower in the neighbor's kitchen garden. But it was not the big lumpish boy and his vulgar pet German Shepherd they saw this time. Instead, a human girl of about sixteen years old appeared, carrying something in her arms. This was Fisko's sister Ivana, and the "something" was an Angora cat. It was Beyza, of course, purring away contentedly in the girl's arms. She smelled as if she had bathed in lavender that morning.

"C'mon now, you little cutie, we're going to buy you a nice studded collar," the girl said. Beyza meowed loudly in protest at the very thought of having to wear a collar. "And we're also going to find you some nice, luxury cat food." Beyza, who could be a fickle, rather spoiled creature, squirmed and purred with pleasure at the mere *mention* of luxury.

The three cats present watched closely as the girl unlatched the front gate. So Beyza was alive, after all. She was also unharmed by boy or dog, which naturally was a tremendous relief to all concerned. Yet, after the happiness at seeing her in one piece, other, more complicated emotions ensued. As far as Magyar and the others could see, the little white cat was being treated like a feline princess. It certainly didn't look as if Beyza was trying to escape. Watching as the girl walked toward the village taking Beyza with her, Magyar didn't know whether to be angry, sad, or both.

"Don't worry, Magyar. We'll get her back," said Felicia.

"Anyway, she will soon get tired of being spoiled," added Dragan, trying to be helpful.

"Beyza? Spoiled? Tiring of?" Magyar gave a bitter, hollow little laugh and then sunk into a silent sulk. This was actually worse than if he'd shouted and rolled around thumping his paws on the ground. He was thinking dolefully about the barn he used to sleep in, about their little spot on the puszta, the Hungarian plains.

"I still know my way back there," he said glumly. Cats, as you may know, are famed for their navigational abilities. They can find their way home anywhere. For a long moment none of the cats knew what to say to Magyar, he looked so despondent.

"C'mon, let's follow and see where she goes," said Felicia. As usual, it was down to the Queen cat not only to come up with practical solutions but also to keep spirits up among the cat clan. Though she loved him deeply, in some respects she longed for a partner to take the place of Dragan, who was useful when it came to hand-to-hand combat but, it sometimes seemed, little else.

4

Something Fishy at Lunch

*Luncheon is served, and it transpires to be
a much more complicated recipe for
misadventure than just simple fish chowder.*

It was a little after midday as three wild cats moved stealthily behind the girl named Ivana, who was walking briskly down the path to the center of the old town. A light breeze brushed over their fur and a foghorn sounded as a ship sailed into the port of Portorose, the more modern-looking seaside resort next door to Piran. It was in the direction of Portorose that Ivana was headed, with Beyza, the white cat, bundled up in her arms. She eventually led the cats— Felicia, Magyar, and Dragan—to a car parked just outside of Piran's old town, which she started up and promptly drove away in, taking Beyza with her.

Beyza was practically the tabby tomcat Magyar's entire reason for living, and now she was in the hands of another.

"She'll be back later, Magyar," said Felicia, the wild cat Queen. "Don't worry." Yet if it's possible for a cat to have a "hangdog" expression, then that's how Magyar looked at that precise moment. But then, something else began to stir inside his old Hungarian tabby constitution. Faintly at first, and then stronger and stronger. No, it wasn't just indignation. It was his appetite, and it was a craving that would brook no refusal. The poor fellow hadn't had a bite since the evening before, and now he was ravenous. Felicia, who had been studying him hard, sensed this change in mood.

"Come on, Magyar, you Hungarian tough nut," she said. "They'll be serving lunch on the promenade any time now."

"I'm sure we will all feel much better on a nice, full stomach," agreed Dragan, the bluff old warrior, thinking as much of his own tummy as anyone else's.

Magyar had to quietly admit that this was indeed sound thinking.

"Tell us a story as we walk, won't you, Dragan?" said Felicia, trying to keep things light. "I thought I knew most of what there was to know about this country. But you never cease to surprise."

Dragan gave a short, gruff laugh. Ever the proud Slovenian, he was glad to oblige with a story. He paused to consider for a moment: "Well, you know our favorite tavern, The Martin Kirpan?"

"Of course."

"Did you know Kirpan was a Slovenian folk hero?"

"That, I didn't."

"Aha! Well, I reckon ol' Martin Kirpan would be turning in his grave if he knew how the tavern built in his name was being run. Kirpan was both a country bumpkin—and one of nature's gentlemen. Unlike the maître d', he was completely above cruelty to animals, such as we! Not only that, there are things about his legend we could all learn from."

"Really?" said Felicia. "Tell us more about this sound fellow!"

"Well, Martin Kirpan was a man of immense strength, who once lifted up his horses as if they were so many chairs. This was to enable the Emperor's carriage to pass by."

Sounding like he had finished his tale, Dragan leaned against a lamppost. He folded his paws and looked somewhat pleased with himself.

"Is that it?" asked Felicia. "Is there supposed to be a moral to this story?"

"Isn't it obvious?" Dragan replied.

"Most definitely not."

"Well, Martin Kirpan was such a heroic type that later on the Emperor called on him to be a Giant Killer."

"And?"

"Well, clearly the point is, sometimes it doesn't pay to draw attention to yourself: You might be asked to kill a giant."

"Oh dear, another one of Dragan's shaggy dog stories," said Magyar, attempting a smile. Dragan more than matched this attempt with one of his great Chartreux cat grins.

It is fair to say the stories Dragan liked to recount were the kind that were told in days gone by. In those days ordinary people believed in ogres and trolls and elves that lived in the forest, in fairy godmothers, and in giants who battled with Dragons. In that now-distant world, fair damsels locked up in the towers of enchanted castles awaited their rescue by valiant-hearted youths who were ready to take on any villain. Somehow also in those far-off times, it seemed that the cleverer were much smarter and the foolish more stupid than in our own day and age. Yet it was also a time where everybody, prince or pauper, wizard or fool, owl or cat, knew a goodly store of tall stories to make a long winter's evening pass pleasantly. For all intents and purposes, Felicia, Dragan, and the wild cats of Piran still lived in that world.

It was the times that had changed, not they.

BY THE TIME THEY GOT TO THE MARTIN KIRPAN TAVERN, the Hungarian tabby was still ravenous but also increasingly furious about the whole situation with Beyza. Why, the more he thought about it, the worse it stuck in his claw. The injustice of it all! He was in an altogether reckless, dangerous mood.

A young human couple was taking coffee with a chocolate cake between them. Magyar's taste buds were on fire, and his anger made him rash. So he did something that no feral cat of Piran was ever supposed to do. He leapt up onto the table, and for a moment, gazed longingly at the chocolate cake sitting between the couple, a youngish man and woman. It looked even better up close: dark, rich melting chocolate, slathered with delicious-looking cream. The temptation was simply too much. Magyar grabbed the cake with both paws and was about to make off with it when the maître d' appeared from nowhere.

The maître d's arms shot out, and he seized the fat Hungarian tabby by the neck and gave it a good squeeze. Strangulation! Why do bullies always instinctively strangle a cat if they get hold of one? Who can say, but it looked like it was all up for the Magyar mongrel from the puszta. And now, in one swift fluid movement, the maître d' bundled Magyar into his arms, holding him close across his chest. This might have been partly because one of his customers was yelling at him to stop, but more likely because he had other plans.

Cat history does record that for thousands of cat years the greatest pleasure of any maître d' of the Martin Kirpan Tavern is when, unobserved by restaurant patrons, he may torment one of the wild cats of Piran. The happy diners in his restaurant always fail to notice the animal cruelty taking place while they sip their wine and chew their fish. Well, almost always.

"Stop hurting him!" the young woman said, just about as firmly as she could.

"Of course, Madame," the maître d' said, in the most patronizing tone imaginable. "The little one will come to no harm. I am going to call the local, how do you say?"

"I don't know, buster, how do you say?"

"The SPCA, yes. That is how you say. I take him now to the SPCA."

And then the maître d' shrieked. Why? Because Felicia had, quite instinctively, lunged at the maître d's leg and dug her claws into his trousers. Somehow he managed to shake Felicia off and, with a kick of his patent leather shoe, sent her flying across the promenade. He still clung to Magyar, who was struggling to free himself, but to no avail. His face a picture of triumph, the maître d' was about to wheel on his heels and go inside. Once in the kitchen, Magyar's life expectancy could not be longer than a few minutes. You will remember the maître d's skill with a meat cleaver.

Watching the drama unfold from under the cover of a tablecloth, Dragan felt like he had to make an awful lot of quick calculations. For one thing, he could just about guess the amount of time Magyar had left to live. Once Magyar was inside that kitchen, alone with the maître d': probably about ten seconds. He would have to be saved, and the only way Dragan could see of doing this was by invoking Majikat. But Felicia was halfway down the promenade, licking her wounds. He wasn't sure she would she approve. Plus, it was daylight, which no cat really likes for practicing Majikat. Also, although there weren't many human people around, there was still that young couple, both of whom, Dragan sensed, had seen right through the wild cats of Piran. Nevertheless, it had to be done. Magyar must be saved! He'd be able to convince Felicia there had been no alternative, because there really hadn't.

The precise instant Dragan began meowing the Majikat Meow, everyone froze. Without exactly knowing what he was doing, the maître d' very quietly, very passively unfolded his arms and let Magyar go. (If he had *known* what he was doing, he wouldn't have done it.) Freed from his clutches, the Hungarian tabby sprinted off as fast as he could in a blaze of fast-moving orange fur. There was the Majikat again, changing the course of events. The spell cast, Dragan now ran hurtling toward the maître d'. But then, a stitch in time before him came Felicia, running up the maître d's trouser legs and onto his waistcoat.

"*Che bravo* (How beautiful), Dragan!" she cried to him. "Well done!" So, she obviously approved of his use of Majikat. Well, that was a relief. Felicia came to a stop on the place just above the maître d's chest where Magyar had been enfolded in his long, wiry arms. There was a long strange moment when the maître d's eyes met with hers.

Who with any natural sympathies or finer feelings could despise such a noble creature as this oriental cat?

Not to mention those eyes, which shone like dewdrops on a lotus leaf. Even the maître d', for just a split second, had to admire the slender animal's dazzling eyes and immaculate coat, the color of midnight.

The maître d' looked quizzical, as if trying to understand his own behavior. But Felicia hadn't quite finished with Gaston the maître d', because then it came: THWACK! A big punch socked to the face, right between the eyes. Instantly, he collapsed onto the floor. Now, it might seem hard to believe that little Felicia's delicate little paw could deliver an almost knockout punch to a human of that size. But perhaps she was still in the Majikat "zone."

Dragan and Magyar just watched, finding it hard not to admire this splendid cleanup operation by their Queen. Felicia held her ground a moment longer. She stared at the maître d', even as he got back on his feet. Then she took a moment to look long and hard at the young couple, whose names were Zach and Niki. Her gaze was hypnotic, and well she knew it. When she blinked, Zach, Niki, and the maître d' alike all felt dazed and confused, unsure about what they had just seen. That of course had been Felicia's intention. She meowed again, softly this time, but with an edge of contempt, and ran away in the direction of Ribiski (Fish) Lane.

The young couple were both struck dumb for a moment. But the black cat's hypnosis was only partially successful: they knew *something* strange had just happened. Just as they were trying to process it

*Felicia and the maître d' eyeball to eyeball.
The moment when the bad-tempered headwaiter
forgets himself, and gets caught up in her eyes.*

all, the maître d' was already back on his feet, flapping his hands in the air and apologizing profusely for:

"This beastly interruption! Really it is unpardonable!"

"What is really unpardonable is you, and the way you treat those poor cats!" said the young woman called Niki. She was quite out of breath with astonishment and emotion. It is also fair to say she had quite strong views on such matters.

"Would you care for any more coffee, Madame?" the maître d' said by way of answer in the most insincerely sincere way imaginable.

"No, thank you," the young man named Zach answered for her, "just the bill please."

From the day it opened in 1714 and for three hundred years, the maître d's at the Martin Kirpan Tavern had lived in a constant state of hostility with the wild cats of Piran. And all because the maître d's were worried that the cats would destroy the "atmosphere and reputation of quality, service, and professionalism" they had "worked so hard to establish" for lo these many years.

Who could really blame them?

IF MAGYAR HAD KNOWN JUST HOW GOOD A TIME Beyza was having, he would have *really* been furious. Mind you, the evening before she had only just avoided some kind of hideous death dreamed up by Fisko, a teenage boy who saw all of life as a very fast and rather brutal video game.

Fortuitously, Fisko's older sister Ivana had been up and about in the villa when he arrived home with Thor slobbering at his side and Beyza wriggling in his backpack. She hadn't been able to sleep, Ivana had said. She had come downstairs and found Fisko in the kitchen. She saw him wrestling the cuddly white cat, about to wring its poor neck. You see? Bullies and cats and strangulation—again! Anyway, upon seeing this, something inside of her snapped.

Call it a sense of common decency, if you will. Or even if you won't.

"Fisko, don't be so stupid. Look at him! He's gorgeous." Humans are notoriously poor at identifying cat gender, but Beyza, who was listening, didn't mind if this nice young girl thought she was a he. As long as there was one human present who wanted to save her! Fisko had growled his response.

"I'm not letting you have it. *You're* the stupid one. Think you are the big boss around here because Mama and Papa are away. I do whatever I want."

"Okay, fine. Do what you want with the cat."

Beyza didn't like the sound of this at all. She let out a perfectly understandable whimper.

"But just know that I'm going to tell Katya and all her friends," Ivana continued, "and they will all know you are a very sad and troubled boy." At the very mention of this girl named Katya, the boy Fisko's whole attitude, posture, and aspect switched down a few gears. Ivana continued on at him.

"So, is this really what you want? For every single girl in town to think you are some kind of sick-o-path," she said, meaning of course to say "psychopath."

The statement had been left hanging in the air for a few seconds, while poor little Beyza wriggled some more and prayed to the moon and the stars above for her deliverance.

"C'mon Fisko, give me the kitten. I'll take care of him."

"You are to tell Katya I gave you this—just so you can give to her."

"Oh, all right. Just give me the kitten, Fisko."

"I don't think it is a kitten; she is fully grown. And it is a she, not a he. But, here, you can have her. For now, but you are to give this cat to Katya Marinovic!"

"Yeah, whatever, Fisko. Go and play some stupid video game or something."

With a final show of stubborn reluctance, Fisko handed the adorable white Angora over to his sister and went sulkily to the garage, taking Thor the German Shepherd with him.

BACK IN THE CRYPT AFTER THAT PERFORMANCE AT LUNCH, Dragan was relieved not to be censured for using his judgment and casting a Majikat spell. There were weeks to go before the new moon. The wild cats would certainly have to ration their use of Majikat until the next lunar cycle. More than three spells, they all believed, would unleash chaos: the delights of paradise, perhaps—but also the terrors of the damned.

Felicia had the good sense to realize that a lecture wouldn't do much good in the case of Magyar. Besides, they were all so very tired. So they did what cats do in such circumstances, when their bellies are full and it's mid-afternoon. They found a quiet spot and fell into a deep sleep. Felicia dreamed that she was the captain of the pirate ship *Fancy,* with a crew made up solely of cats—the wild cats of Piran. Magyar dreamed of Beyza, of course, running across a wheat field on the Hungarian puszta. Dragan had a dream in which Martin Kirpan was brought back to life, wandered into the Martin Kirpan Tavern, and proceeded to tear the place apart—completely—using only his bare hands.

You may not be aware of it, but the average cat sleeps around sixteen hours a day. As must be plain, the wild cats of Piran were never average in any way. But they slept around sixteen hours a day, anyway. (Everything else you read about here happens in the seven or eight hours a day when they are awake.) After such rich dreaming, all of the cats woke up and then ate some more—before going back to sleep again for a while. This time, however, it was a dreamless sleep. They were in a realm so dark, thick, and obscure that it defies description.

Except of course to say: "*Purrrrrrrrrrrrrrrrrzzzzzzzzzzzzzzzzzzzzzzz.* . . ."

However, it would be well for readers of this chronicle to remember that if General Rat ever slept, it was with one eye open. So we'd best keep *our* eyes open, for we definitely have not seen the last of him.

5

Night Visions

Dragan goes on a midnight stroll and is witness to not only an unbelievable scene but also language that makes his whiskers curl.

I t was late afternoon, and Felicia, Dragan, and Magyar had just had a long nap. When they awoke, they all had one thing in common. That is to say, they were all hungry. But deciding to avoid the restaurant promenade, they made their way to the home of a magnificent, stout Italian woman named Signora Fortuna. (This means "Lady Luck" in Italian, and that's certainly how the cats all thought of her.)

Sure enough, here she was at 47 Boniface Lane, and it was as if she had been waiting for them. This fine, generous woman was wearing a white frilly apron over a dress that would have already been out of fashion in the 1970s, and a pair of ancient but sturdy house slippers. As she swept her doorstep she sang the tune of a love song she'd learned as a young girl but whose words she'd later forgotten. Signora Fortuna seemed to be perpetually watering the plants and sweeping the mat on the terrace outside her home. Yet inside, the house must have been a hive of activity, too, for there were usually sheets and pillowcases hanging on her balcony; and, almost always, the smell of good cooking wafted from her kitchen. Her friendly manner aside, it was these delicious aromas that brought the wild cats of Piran back time and time again to her cozy little landing.

"*Buon giorno!* (Good day!) Well if it isn't my favorite little animals. I've got a nice fish stew I can let you have a little of today, if that sounds good, my dears." All three cats nodded their heads in unison and licked their paws. Signora Fortuna smiled broadly, not seeing anything the least bit strange in the psychic connection she had with the feral cats of her hometown.

Soon, an impromptu luncheon was served along with generous saucers of milk, all consumed in grateful silence by Felicia, Dragan, and Magyar. Each cat was thinking the same thing: how unpredictable these human beings could be! Why, they were almost as complicated as cats sometimes—cruel and barbaric like the teenage boy Fisko, or the maître d' at the Kirpan Tavern. But then, just occasionally, how nice they could be too: like some of the young waiters at the Fontana Restaurant in Piran, who even fed them scraps, or dear old Signora Fortuna with her potluck lunches.

It really was rather baffling.

IT WAS WELL THEY HAD A GOOD MEAL, for several of the wild cats of Piran had a long night ahead of them. They were, you will doubtless agree, a pretty fearless sort of a crew, with the occasional exception of Magyar. The most obviously warlike of their number was Dragan, but that evening he too saw something that gave even him pause.

The tough old Slovene Chartreux cat was tiptoeing clumsily along a cobblestone roof on his hind legs and feeling content with the entire world, or at least the entire world of Piran. He was a cat in the night on a cool tile roof, feeling good about his place in the grand scheme of things, as we should all do from time to time.

"Gaze at the winged lion!" He smiled to himself as he recalled the slogan Felicia had been chanting, just a few nights before, right before she had saved his life.

"Gaze at the winged lion that grasps territories, seas, and stars." Dragan said it softly to himself and to no other. He had to admit, it felt good, perhaps because all cats dream of flying, even if they won't admit it out loud.

All of a sudden, a strange sound carried on the night air brought him to a sudden stop. Careful not

to make any noise, he bolted across the tiles onto
the gutters. This was a better place from which to
observe May 1 Piazza, or the "small piazza," as it
is also known. Down below him on the piazza was
a most peculiar vision, and to Dragan, or any other
cat, a most decidedly alarming one. The whole piazza, the entire square, was filled with—there is no
other word for it—rats. Dozens and dozens of rats:
does and bucks (female and male), brown rats and
black rats, young rats, old rats, rats who were little
larger than mice, and rats who were nearly as big
as cats.

They were lined up in ranks on the square, all
facing a smaller group of rats that stood above them.
These rats had hoisted themselves up onto the large,
stone rainwater cistern and the two statues of cher-
ubs that stand together on May 1 Piazza. There was
something military about the entire arrangement.

Mind you, they were all twitching and sniveling
and sniffing like rats always do. And yet by rat standards, they were a disciplined body of troops. They
were also a captive audience. Now so too was Dragan,
as he listened in while the rat leader addressed the
rat rabble. For there *was* a rat leader, that much was
clear. He was a burly-looking specimen with an eye
patch.

What the rat leader—General Rat, of course—
had to say was completely unintelligible, at least as
far as Dragan was concerned. You see, like most cats,
Dragan didn't speak or understand a word of Rat. He

had absolutely no interest in doing so, either. But whatever the irate leader was saying, plainly it was strong stuff; for in no time it whipped up the twitching mass of rodents into a fever. Together as one, the Rat Army began chanting a slogan. Whenever the General finished a particularly emotional passage of rat oratory, its troops called out it in unison.

"Ukwbyg!!! Jqhsdp!!!" they cried. "Ukwbyg!!! Jqhsdp!!!"

Except for a few cats with a specialist's knowledge of, and interest in, languages, most cats couldn't tell you how to say "Hello" in Rat, let alone something like "Tomorrow! Victory!"—which, dear, heart-palpitating reader, is precisely what the rats were chanting: "Ukwbyg!!! Jqhsdp!!!"

But Dragan was no fool, even if he acted the part from time to time. He listened hard and made a mental note of their anthemic chant:

"Ukwbyg!!! Jqhsdp!!!"

You see, there was one wild cat in the town of Piran who would be able to translate. His name was Leopold, and he was a Japanese Bobtail cat from Vienna. Among his other talents, Leopold was a philologist, which means that he was an expert in languages. In Human, he could understand and mimic German, Slovene, Italian, Turkish, and English. He knew snippets of many animal languages too. There was just one problem with consulting Leopold. He was an outcast, at least as far as Felicia was concerned.

Suffice it to say, among all the potential dangers faced by the wild cats of Piran, including the maître d' and that nasty hoodlum Fisko, there was one that they would ignore at their peril. That danger, of course, was the rats of Piran. And where, you might ask, were they? Well, the answer to that is that they were *everywhere*.

Dozens, nay, hundreds of wild rats slept in underground burrows they had dug themselves in the hills above Piran. Some were next to villas like the one Fisko lived in. Some stowed away in fishing boats and lived an adventurous-sounding life going from port to port, with Piran as their base. Not that many of them would have identified their lives as adventurous, or exciting, or boring, or anything else. Their ability to reflect on such matters was very limited indeed.

Human scientific opinion suggests that rats are one of the most intelligent species in the animal realm. But that's because few human scientists have ever engaged a rat in conversation. Were they to do so, they might realize that rats are actually very dull creatures indeed. A typical example of rat social intercourse might run something like this:

RAT 1	"I want that bit of lettuce."
RAT 2	"I want that bit of lettuce."
RAT 1	"No, *I* want that bit of lettuce."
RAT 3	"I want a bit of that lettuce, too."
RAT 1	"I want a bit of that lettuce."

And so on. This would be one of their more stimulating conversations. You've already heard some of the rat language: "Vfpuaj, Mzhdrb," and so on. Not easy listening, by any stretch of the imagination. But "Ukwbyg!!! Jqhsdp!!!"—what did that mean? Dragan thought it important to find out.

When Dragan shared what he had seen with the rest of the colony, he was at first greeted with derision. After all, rats holding a rally on May 1 Piazza, listening to a speech by some kind of rat leader—the very idea! Indeed, Magyar rocked back and forth with laughter, holding his sides.

"A rat leader! That's a good one, Dragan. Tell us another." Mind you, Magyar was borderline hysterical, anyway, without Beyza at his side to calm him down.

This was one disadvantage of Dragan telling so many shaggy dog stories: he had to work twice as hard to be taken seriously at times. Later, after he discussed with Felicia what he had seen and heard, Dragan broached the difficult subject of Leopold. Dragan, in truth, was not particularly fond of the cat Leopold. However, he also knew that he himself was a doer, not a thinker. Thinking—that was Leopold's specialty.

"Felicia," he whispered to her, "there's only one cat in this town who can tell us what 'Ukwbyg!!! Jqhsdp!!!' means. And that's your favorite Viennese snob, Leopold."

"Snob? Leopold? Hmm. *Snob* implies that it is he who shuns *us*, and not the other way around."

"As you like it, Queenie. But while we stand here discussing the finer points of cat protocol, those vermin are up to no good. Wouldn't it be good to find out what it is?" Felicia thought to herself that Dragan had a very good point, but that's not quite how it came out.

"It does sound to me as if the rats are getting ideas above their station," she said. "And yes, perhaps also it is time Leopold and I had a chat."

Ah, Felicia and Leopold. They had once been so close, perhaps because they were so alike. And then they had drifted apart, possibly for the same reason. Lithe, lean, and active, the Japanese Bobtail called Leopold had come down to Piran for a weekend with his Viennese "owners" a few years ago. He had met the wild cats of Piran and had quickly fallen for the call of the wild. And, truth be told, he had fallen for Felicia and she for him. Yet later they had fallen out—and it was all over a ghost. A ghost, you say? That's right, inquisitive reader: your eyes did not deceive you. It had been over a ghost.

Now, have you ever noticed how a cat, in the middle of slumber, will suddenly become watchful, alert, clawing at the air with its paws? How she will seem hyperaware of something going on in the room, of a phantom that seems to exist only in her imagination? Well, of course this isn't something only in the dear creature's mind. It is, in most cases, a ghost. And Piran? Oh, Piran was full of them.

The town of Piran's most famous son was a violin player named Giuseppe Tartini. He was famed in history as the composer of a bewitching piece of music called *The Devil's Trill* Sonata. It was Tartini's statue that stood on the main piazza. On that same square was Tartini House. Leopold, who was as fanatical about music as any true Viennese cat, had taken to climbing up into the attic room of that building, all the better to hear Tartini's ghost play violin.

All along Felicia had disapproved of this, for reasons she could not easily put into words. Then one evening she had been scampering along the rooftop of the violinist's house and saw something that disturbed her. It was only a flickering vision, but she was sure she had glimpsed a demon through the skylight. That's right, a demon, with a horned head, a pointed beard, the feet of a goat, and the wings of a vampire bat. A chill ran down her spine, and every ounce of her intuition told her the wild cats must be ordered to stay away from Tartini's ghost.

She instructed Leopold not to visit the old violin player anymore. But he disobeyed time and time again. The two cats quarreled, and Leopold, who was something of a loner by nature, went his own way. He had stopped passing by the crypt many months ago. When they passed each other in the street, Felicia would pretend not to see him, and he would return the compliment.

But now—with this strange gathering on May 1 Piazza, and with "Ukwbyg!!! Jqhsdp!!!"—it was indeed time for Felicia to swallow her pride, even if her

Leopold listens rapturously as the ghost of Giuseppe Tartini plays violin. Felicia skulks in the background.

pride was an uncomfortable ball of fur to digest, and seek out the wily Viennese cat.

IT WAS THE VERY EARLY HOURS OF THE MORNING in the crypt, an hour when only cats, owls, ghosts, and the occasional storybook writer should be awake.

"Beyza, my ooooooooooooooh . . ." This was Magyar, lying in a heap on top of a coffin and practically sobbing. Atop the long pinewood box had been carved the unmistakable figure of a knight in shining armor. Felicia paced up and down on its contours. Magyar was carrying on, feeling terribly sorry for himself.

"Unfair terribly, deserve not I," he sobbed.

"Good no do you whimpering!" Felicia snapped, imitating his back-to-front way of speaking Cat. "Let's try and be practical and think of a solution." This might sound harsh on the part of Felicia, but Magyar had been laying it on a bit thick. Only after eating and sleeping equally solidly for several hours had he then remembered to be thoroughly miserable about Beyza's imprisonment.

"You might have to get used to being a bachelor again, Magyar," said Dragan, swinging his body along the old silver handles of another coffin.

"If she has picked up bad habits, is it me of because, I mean, it's because of me," said Magyar to no one in particular. "I taught her everything she knows about being a feral cat." It all came out in a flood of tears and self-recrimination—mixed with self-justification. It had been Beyza's idea to leave the puszta, the Hungarian plains, and now she was a prisoner, or worse! Why had she not listened to Magyar? Because if he'd had his way, they would still be on the puszta, feasting on field mice and pancakes and jam and ham and cheese, and sleeping in a nice, comfortable barn!

"Good is straw of bed!" Magyar exclaimed.

"You're quite finished then, are you?" asked Dragan, while Magyar took a breath.

"What you both need to do is calm down," Felicia said with conviction. "Besides, Magyar, the girl was seen returning to Dogboy Villa with Beyza a few hours ago. We've all heard the purring coming from in there. To me it certainly doesn't sound like Beyza is dead." All the other cats fell quiet and brooded for a bit, as they tended to do when Felicia asserted her natural authority. This feral cat from Naples, who could be as regal as any Queen, now addressed her subjects in the underground tomb they called home.

"My fellow felines!" she began. "From what Dragan has told us about the rat army, we must now be on the highest possible state of alert. The incident at lunch today was also the second time in this lunar cycle that one of our band has used Majikat. According to the old, unwritten rules we may employ it just once more between now and the new moon. More than that, and we're in for a bumpy ride. But then, we wild cats do not shrink from danger or a challenge, do we?"

"No, no, no!" the others were quick to respond.

"Indeed," Felicia continued, "I believe if you asked each and every one of us if we would trade our destitute existence for one of safe domestic comfort then we would say . . ."

Magyar took over at this point, unable to contain himself. "Then we would say, to a cat, 'not for all the fish in all the waterfront restaurants on the Adriatic Sea, or all the sacks full of dead rats in the world.'"

"Well put, Prince Magyar!" It was true. He'd managed the whole thing without speaking backward. As glum as he was, Magyar still entertained the notion that he was the leader. The wild cats' real leader, Felicia, for once allowed him to persist in this delusion. But she added another warning, instructing the wild cats to travel in pairs at all times.

"The only safety we can expect to enjoy right now is safety in battle, and so there's absolutely no point in splitting ourselves up. We must stick together. Travel with at least one other cat by your side, at all times, day and night. All for one and one for all, as I believe someone once said."

"Oh, undoubtedly," noted Dragan, in his usual droll way.

Then Felicia turned her magnetic gaze on the lovelorn Hungarian tabby cat. "Magyar, you come along with me; there's something I'd like you to have a look at. *Si? Andiamo*! (Yes? Let's go!)" Felicia was well known for these late-night walks and talks, the point of which was sometimes lost on her fellow felines. But not on this night, young dreamers—oh no, not on this night.

6

The Lady in Waiting

*Felicia proves herself to be a Renaissance cat,
even if she was born a century later, into the
Age of Enlightenment. And we are introduced to
the enigmatic Viennese cat, Leopold.*

On Piazza Tartini, the center of medieval Piran, a few doors down from Tartini House, stands the Benečanka House, which in Slovene means the "Venetian Woman's House." This house, or "palazzo," was actually built for a woman from Piran, by a wealthy trader from Venice, and in the Venetian style. In its day, which was 600 years ago, it was called the Venetian Merchant's House, and if it was good enough back then, it will suffice for us now—the Venetian Merchant's House it shall be known as hitherto. With its rose-colored exterior, it is still the oldest, smartest, and quite the *pinkest* house on the whole piazza, even at two in the morning. The windows of the house are quite distinctively Venetian, with ornate white stone decorations.

There is a plaque on the wall, upon which is engraved a winged lion with a scroll running from its mouth. The inscription on the scroll reads: "*Lassa pur dir*." This is Latin for "let them all talk." There is also a balcony on the corner of the house, a balcony upon which you might quite reasonably expect to see a damsel in distress, or a Juliet, looking for her Romeo. Felicia had escorted Magyar to a spot on the piazza facing the beautiful rose-colored palazzo.

"Now," she whispered, "we must just watch very carefully. I've never known her to appear to anyone but me. Well, that's perhaps because I've never shown anyone this. But maybe we'll be lucky." Her eyes gleamed in the dark.

"Never known *who* to appear?"

"Shhhhh!"

All of a sudden there was movement, or at least a play of light suggesting movement, on the balcony of the Venetian Merchant's House. A woman with long, golden locks and a beautiful silk dress now appeared, as if from nowhere. She was very comely, even to a cat's way of thinking. This golden maiden had a pained expression on her face and held out her arms in front of her.

"Beautiful she is," gasped Magyar. "I mean, for a human-type person!"

"Well, yes, quite."

"What is she doing?"

"She's doing the same thing she does every night. She is waiting for *him* to arrive."

"Hmm? I mean him—him is who, I mean, who is . . . ?"

"Yes, Magyar, I know what you mean." Felicia continued, in the quietest whisper imaginable: "The story goes that a maiden from Piran fell in love with a wealthy trader from the most serene city. This merchant of Venice built a house in Piran for his lady-love. The very romantic-looking balcony was specially constructed so that the maiden from Piran could wait and could wave to him every time the merchant of Venice's ship pulled into the harbor."

"So why she is still waiting? I mean, after six hundred years."

"That, I do not know, Magyar. What I do know is this: she waits for him on that balcony at the same time every night." Magyar looked again at the woman, into the liquid pools of her blue eyes, studying her gestures. He recognized the longing, the love, the despair. It was not unlike the way the Hungarian tabby felt whenever he thought of Beyza. Still he examined the maid. She really was a beauteous damsel, even in distress. Distress—at once that emotion seemed to give way to another as her eyes lit up and a great smile spread across her face.

"What's this? Does she see his ship? But that . . ."

Magyar didn't have time to finish, for without warning, the beautiful maiden's smile, and then her ghostly image, disappeared. It all happened in two very fast shakes of a cat's tail.

"Then happened what?" shrieked Magyar. "Humph, I mean, what happened then?"

"I don't know," answered the sleek black Queen cat. "Every time I've seen her, she disappears at precisely the same time. But the point in showing you this is that she never gives up."

"Eh?"

"She who waits on the balcony, was she not a mere, one-life human mortal at one time? And what human could ever outlast a cat when it comes to patience, eh?"

"True is that nobody knows how to wait for something like a cat!" said Magyar. A tiny ray of optimistic sunshine had pierced the clouds of gloom.

"So you mustn't give up, either, my stout Magyar friend. Isn't there the heart of a Hungarian hussar beating inside that manly feline breast?"

"Of course there is! 'Regiment and the honor!' I mean: 'honor and the regiment!'"

"So then, cheer up and act like a *tom*! We all know Beyza is alive, and we all know she's being looked after by that girl."

"Looked after? Rot! Escape trying is Beyza . . . She is trying . . ."

"Yes, that's right, Magyar. Beyza is trying to escape, and we're going to help her. But first there's someone I have to see."

The lady in waiting on the balcony of the Venetian House.

FELICIA WAS ONLY DOING WHAT SHE FELT WAS HER DUTY: doing her best to keep Magyar's spirits from flagging. The silly puss had four or five lives of experience to draw upon, so why did he have to be such a ninny?

After seeing Magyar back to the crypt, Felicia did something she wasn't completely proud of. It was something, however, that she thought necessary for the safety of the colony. That is to say, she sneaked into Signora Fortuna's kitchen while the old lady was asleep. She climbed up into her pantry, which was abundant with provender, herbs and spices, and all manner of good things. Felicia searched meticulously until she found what she was looking for: mint. You see, peculiar as it may seem, there's almost nothing rats hate more than the smell of mint. Mint? But that has such a refreshing, wholesome aroma, you say. This may be why rats, who thrive on filth and disease, find the smell of mint so nauseating, disgusting little beasts that they are.

At last, in brown paper packaging, among a lot of other herbs in brown paper bags, Felicia was able to pick out and isolate its fresh, tangy aroma. There was an abundance of mint in the bag, as there seemed to be an abundance of everything in Signora Fortuna's kitchen. Felicia felt bad about stealing anything from that redoubtable and kind lady, who gave so much to the wild cats of Piran. It was, however, for a good cause—the cause of survival. She very deftly placed everything back as it was, or as nearly so as she could manage, and then slipped out the same way she had come, by the kitchen window. Shimmying down a drainpipe, she discovered Dragan waiting for her, a bemused expression on his face.

"What are you doing here? I don't like being followed," she said, embarrassed to be discovered stealing from Signora Fortuna's larder.

"Well, Queenie, I noticed that you saw Magyar back home to safety. But I thought to myself, who's going to look after you? Besides, I've spotted Leopold. He's down at Cape Madonna, getting ready to watch the sun come up, I suppose."

"That sounds like Leopold. He always was a romantic."

"That, I wouldn't know," said Dragan, sounding a little embarrassed. "Well, come on then."

Felicia knew better than to argue with Dragan when he was right about something important, as he was now. The two of them gamboled along until they came to the very tip of the peninsula that jutted out into the sea, the aforementioned Cape Madonna. And, sure enough, there was Leopold. Neat, compact, and spotless in appearance as always, he seemed unsurprised by their arrival. It was as if he had been waiting for them all along.

There was, however, something else waiting for the wild cats, something terrible, just below sea level. An entire swarm of rats was down there, all of them holding their breath, waiting for the signal to attack. That's something you might not know about rats. Your so-called *Rattus norvegicus* (aka Norway rat, brown rat) can swim for hundreds of meters at a time, dive a long way down, and hold its breath for as long as fifteen minutes.

But these particular submariner rats wouldn't even have to wait *that* long for action.

MEANWHILE, UP ON THE HILLS OF PIRAN, IN DOGBOY VILLA, Beyza the white puffball cat was watching television and thinking what a waste of time it all was—television, that is.

It was hard on her eyes, and it didn't feed or cuddle or play with her. It didn't teach you anything much, either. TV was, perhaps surprisingly, something Beyza really could have done without. Worse, just like her brother, Fisko, this girl Ivana was often awake in the wee hours of the morning: the time when most humans have the decency to be asleep! Cats like their privacy, especially at that hour.

Mind you, Ivana wasn't a bad human girl in her way, but she did listen to a lot of very loud and monotonous music, and she talked or sent messages on something called a smartphone practically every hour of the day or night. She also had at least two annoying friends who came over and talked nonstop for hours. When they weren't talking too much, they always tried to tickle Beyza's belly—something Beyza didn't particularly care for. A very fickle and sometimes contrary cat was she.

Moreover, Beyza had started missing the gang and Magyar—probably in that order, truth be told.

She missed being with her own kind, and who could blame the rather simple but high-maintenance little creature? The villa would do for another day or two, she thought, but she also had to find an escape route. Since she was a lazy cat, it would be best, or so she thought, if she could find an ally within the villa to help plan her escape and ensure that it would go smoothly.

An accomplice of this nature she would indeed find, but in the most unlikely of quarters.

BACK AT CAPE MADONNA, FELICIA HAD A LONG, hard look at her old friend. She really was very glad to see him. Well, for one thing, Leopold was "easy on the eyes." A particularly well-assembled Japanese Bobtail cat, he could leap several feet in the air effortlessly and took great pride in his cleanliness and appearance. Even after three years in the wild, Leopold retained many of the habits and mannerisms of a domesticated cat from an orderly household in Vienna. But still waters run deep, as they say. In his own way, Leopold was passionate—about the sea, about music, and, though he wouldn't admit it, about Felicia.

"*Guten morgen* (Good morning)," he said in Human German. "What a pleasure to see you both." So far, so good. But then: "Come to apologize?" This, you will agree, did *not* bode so well.

"Dragan," said Felicia, "let's leave this loner to his own devices. That's clearly how he likes it."

"I'm sorry, Felicia," replied Leopold. "It's been a long time." That was more like it.

"Come on, then, you two, kiss and make up," said Dragan in his gruff way. "You know you want to." So the two old friends rubbed faces for an unusually long period of time. Poor old Dragan didn't know where to look.

"I've missed you," Leopold said softly. "I've even missed *you,* Dragan. Can you believe that?"

"Not without difficulty."

"We have all missed each other," said Felicia, quite reasonably. "And we'd like your help with something, Leopold," she admitted, which by her standards was a real climb down. She and Dragan then explained about the rats gathering on May 1 Piazza. "They were chanting something," said Dragan. "It went 'Ukwbyg!!! Jqhsdp!!!'"

"'Ukwbyg!!! Jqhsdp!!!,' eh?" said the Viennese cat, suddenly all business. Because although Leopold felt roughly the same way about Rat as many Frenchmen feel about the English language, he could actually understand some Rat words and phrases.

"'Ukwbyg!!! Jqhsdp!!!' My, but it's an ugly language. The gist of it, I think, would be 'tomorrow, death.' And implied in that: death-to-the-cats-who-for-far-too-long-have-been-top-dog. It sounds to me like these dirty rats are up to no good, and will have to be stopped," Leopold concluded.

"One stinking rodent at a time," as Dragan put it, smiling his eerie grimace and looking forward to battle. "In the good old days we used to bite the heads off rats. Have you forgotten that?" He laughed as he said it, and so did Felicia and Leopold. "All you do is grab the rat in the area where its neck should be, and disgusting as it may seem to you, you bite that loathsome little mite's head off. Yum, yum, yum, yummity yum yum. Bite its head off and chew, chew, chew," Dragan said between imaginary mouthfuls, then: "Garumph, garumph, garumph! Gulp, digest, and 'buuuuwww- waaaaaaaaaarpp!'" Then, finally, "Oh my, that tasted good!" Felicia's and Leopold's sides were now aching, they were laughing so much.

"So now, you leave them rats to me," added Dragan. "The rest of you might be too proud and dainty to bite off a rat's head—and eat the rest of him with jam—but old Dragan ain't," he snorted.

All at once another voice joined in the conversation. It was a chilling, mechanical-sounding grind of a voice.

"Your translation isn't quite correct. The phrase is, 'tomorrow, victory,' not 'tomorrow, death.' But you grasped the meaning of it."

Three pairs of cats' eyes swerved toward the ugly great rodent that had snuck up on them, seemingly from nowhere. It was General Rat, of course, standing there on the rocks, eye patch in place, whiskers twitching contemptuously. (The General's whiskers could do that.)

Even as the General was talking, other rats, all of them soaking wet, began scurrying up from underneath the waterline. As you will recall, they had been hiding there and holding their breath for several minutes. Soon, dozens of the unpleasant little blighters had massed around the three wild cats. Though they did a good job of not showing it, Felicia, Dragan, and Leopold were all rather startled. And quite justifiably so. The rats began moving toward them in formation, or in what Egyptian cats would have called a Phalanx. In the rat tongue this would have been known as a "Jbrdqa." Most things in Rat are known as a "Jbrdqa" of one kind or another, but let's not get off on too much of a tangent about that, now shall we?

Not when our beloved Piranese cats face extinction at the tooth and claw of such an unpleasant grouping! The mind recoils in horror! But instead of rushing them all at once, the whole tensely convulsing bunch came to a halt fifteen or twenty centimeters away. General Rat puffed himself up to his full height and again he spoke, in very rough but not incomprehensible Cat. (Remember, by rat standards, the General was not only an officer but also a gentleman and a scholar.)

"Look ye, we come not to attack you. Well, not much. Instead, we are here to warn you. To let you know that the rules are changing; and that from now on, you wild cats are no longer the top of the food chain. We wild rats are!"

"What's this?!" growled Dragan, who was at that moment even more indignant than he was afraid.

"You will have to live with *us*. Not the other way around. Not anymore."

"Ho-ho-ho." Again, this was Dragan. "You're funny, did you know that?" He laughed and then glared at General Rat.

That Chartreux smile of Dragan's really was rather alarming. Leopold, on the other paw, tried to employ reason. He was raised in Vienna, after all, that city of international diplomacy.

"Surely an armed confrontation isn't necessary? I always find a good healthy debate to be helpful. Why don't we organize one now?" He was of course playing for time, for all the good that would do him. Ignoring Leopold completely, the General continued.

"There are some things we rats are not going to put up with anymore. Number one, being eaten. Two, being killed. Three, er, no, actually I think that's about it. No killing rats, no eating them. Of course, we'll have to kill one of you now and leave the others alive to tell the tale, just to send a clear message."

"Come on, rat-leader-type. Let's at least be accurate," said Felicia, herself playing for time. "It's not so often that we eat rats these days. In fact I'd say you're off the menu for most of the cats I know." Yet even as Felicia tried to stall, Dragan was fairly sure *he* was the one wild cat these rats would choose to make an example of. Dragan's reaction was predictable. He was absolutely livid.

"Do you mind if I go first?" he said, smiling of course and stepping forward. As far as he was concerned, it was as good a time as any for a pitched battle.

7

The Battle of Cape Madonna

---

*Battle ensues, and cat-rat rivalry for supremacy
is expressed in no uncertain terms. There is an
unpredictable intervention from a species not usually
thought of as involved in these affairs.*

It was just before dawn on the Istrian coastline of Slovenia, in the charming little town of Piran. Yet for three wild cats of Piran, there was no time to waste admiring the scenery or the sunrise. Felicia, Dragan, and Leopold faced their implacable enemy with courage: the terrible wild rats of Piran and their leader, General Rat. Ever the warrior, Dragan was the first to act. In one swift, animal movement he grabbed one of the larger rats in the front row, picked him up, and threw him over his shoulders, sending him tumbling and squeaking about fifteen meters out to sea. He did as much without thinking. If Dragan had thought it over, he would have remembered that the sea holds few terrors for a rat.

"Dragan! That's no good; that's where they came from!" Felicia reminded him.

"Very well, I'll try another approach." Dragan's paw shot out and he grabbed another rat, and was about to wring its neck. Well, General Rat wasn't going to stand for this, and both Felicia and Leopold knew it.

The twitching body of rats braced themselves for a battle. "*Nctohw*! (Charge!)" the General bellowed as loud as he could. They were rats. They took orders. They charged.

Dragan, it could be said, was equal to the moment, for here was an encounter that was red in tooth and claw. It was rather grotesque and gruesome, as nature in the raw can be. Inspired, Felicia reached forward, grabbing another rat in her agile little paw. "D'you know, *amico* (friend) Dragan, I think you might have the right idea."

Confronted by vastly superior numbers of a species they considered vastly inferior, Felicia, Dragan, and Leopold were still determined to hold their ground. But they were so outnumbered that the rats' victory seemed assured. It was only a matter of time.

IT IS INTERESTING TO NOTE THAT ALTHOUGH DRAGAN was fond of telling old Slovene folk stories about a legendary figure named Martin Kirpan, he was at best only

vaguely aware that his own great-grandfather had inspired one of the oldest Slovene folktales of them all.

The story involving Dragan's great-grandfather
"Zvonimir" was all about a cat that had singlehand-
edly solved an entire village's pest or rodent problem.
Zvonimir had done so by devouring every single rat,
mouse, and gopher in the village and surrounding
countryside. The townspeople, who were simple folk,
were at first delighted. But by the time the wild and
woolly cat had got rid of the very last vermin, the vil-
lagers became frightened that the greedy little beast
would now start eating *them*. And so they offered old
Zvonimir a fish that had been caught in Piran, quite
unsure whether he would touch it or not.

When the cat happily ate the whole fish, including its tail, the people heaved a huge sigh of relief,
and believe you me, they kept the fish coming for
year-after-year to come to the cat sitting at the table.
It was an alarming-looking beast, with wild whiskers
and a rather disturbing smile.

Eventually, after expiring a few times from an
over-stimulated palate, or from choking on fish bones,
Zvonimir simply disappeared one night, and was
thought dead. Yet in the middle of all this gluttony
the old fellow had somehow managed to sire a litter of
kittens, the oldest of which turned out to be Dragan's
grandfather.

Dragan carried those genes in his blood: he could
be vicious when roused, and his appetites knew no
bounds. In light of the threats the cats faced from rats

in modern-day Piran, these attributes could be considered very handy indeed.

AN ANECDOTE CONCERNING DRAGAN'S ANCESTRY seemed a more pleasant way for you, dear reader, to pass the time, than for us to focus on the rather grisly cat-rat battle going on at the tip of Cape Madonna that morning.

And so, rather than giving the reader's delicate sensibilities any more jolts with graphically violent descriptions of the battle, let us just say this: Dragan and the others had fought bravely. But as was inevitable, the rodents were now beginning to overpower them. Leopold was the first to go down, which meant rats were now swarming over his body, and he could depend upon being torn to pieces and eaten in seconds flat. "What a desperately ugly way to go," he thought to himself.

Then, finally, Felicia remembered her errand of earlier that morning. She reached for some leaves of mint she'd been concealing under her belly and crushed them between her teeth, hissing as she did so. The rats backed away at once, repelled by what to humans may be a clean, refreshing odor but to rats is a revolting smell. She quickly passed a bundle of mint leaves to Dragan. "Just bite down hard on the leaves and hiss in your normal fashion!" Dragan did so, watching with amusement as the sheer smell of the stuff worked on the rat nervous system.

"Just like garlic and vampires," he reflected. Leopold managed to get back on his feet, and then he too bit down hard on the mint, releasing more of the odor into the crisp morning air. The rats were falling back, coughing and spluttering like soldiers under attack from mustard gas.

"Aaaaaaqqqqqkkkkkkvvvvvv!!!" they called out in horror and disgust. Many instinctively retreated, and a couple of them actually fainted because of the smell. But not General Rat—who instead berated his troops:

"*Nctohw*! (Charge!)" I said, "*Nctohw!*" The rats looked at each other for a moment, their beady eyes wiggling and their whiskers twitching faster than usual. They didn't appear hugely enthusiastic. "*Nctohw!*" General Rat roared again in his unpleasant tongue.

This was it. This was the window of opportunity for the wild cats. They pushed aside a couple of rats and began running toward the embankment, toward the crypt, toward safety.

OF COURSE, FELICIA WAS DELIGHTED WITH THIS OUTCOME, and even wondered for a moment why she had felt the need to consult Leopold. But then she turned and saw him running alongside her, immaculate in his tuxedo-patterned coat. She was, after all, glad to have him around again. While it cannot be said that this was a conclusive victory over the rats, it was a lucky escape.

And then something happened to make the rats' trouncing complete. You won't have forgotten Zach and Niki, surely? They were the young couple who

The nice young human couple Niki and Zach chase away the rats at the end of the battle of Cape Madonna.

objected to the maître d' and the way he mistreated the wild cats at the Martin Kirpan Tavern. Well, Zach and Niki had woken up and got out of bed especially early that morning, even before sunrise. They were taking a stroll when they spied the conflagration between rat and cat down on the tip of the peninsula. As soon as they saw what was going on, they began barreling toward Cape Madonna. They were both reasonably fit. They were also extremely large from a rat perspective and moving at a fair clip. And Zach had the presence of mind to stop long enough to pick up a rock and throw it at the rats.

Niki was quick to catch on, and soon she too had picked up a rock and thrown it. The rats didn't like the look of this at all. They liked it less when Niki and Zach ran still closer and doubled their efforts, bringing a hail of rocks down upon them. Zach, as it turned out, had a pretty decent aim, the result of his days on the cricket pitch, and he knocked several rats squealing into the sea.

General Rat turned to one of his colonels, and they both squeaked at the other rats, "Kwfnpl!" which in Rat meant, roughly, "Hold your ground, gentlemen. We need fear neither feline nor human, now that I am at your side."

After considering this advice for a few seconds, every single common garden rat began disappearing quickly, scrambling across the rocks to safety, diving into the sea, or otherwise making for cover. By the time the human couple had got to the end of the cape, even General Rat had done the same thing; he had jumped into the water and swum for it.

Like rats leaving a sinking ship, you might say.

ZACH AND NIKI EXCHANGED A LOOK that seemed to suggest they had made their minds up—that the best place to be was gone from there. They began walking briskly away from Cape Madonna and in the general direction of their hotel. Just before they reached the promenade, lined with all those waterfront restaurants including the Martin Kirpan Tavern, they came to Vegova Lane and made a sharp right turn, into the agreeable maze of streets comprising the body of the old town. At the corner of Vegova and Boniface they alighted upon the trio of wild cats, taking a moment to catch their breaths in the cool, early morning shade of Signora Fortuna's porch.

Cats and humans regarded each other for a moment. Their eyes met. There was a glimmer of understanding. Perhaps some intimate vibration, some transmission of gratitude was exchanged. But you started making friends and being grateful to humans—and look where that led! *Domesticity*, for one thing, and that was unacceptable to a feral cat of Piran. Shaking her head almost violently, Felicia began running very, very fast. She whipped between Zach's feet, quite startling him and almost throwing him off-balance. Dragan was as quick to run past Niki, his tail brushing her leg as he sped by. Leopold followed, running as fast as he could.

And the well-intentioned humans? Well, Zach regained his balance and Niki her composure. They both felt as if the cats had been, somehow, rather ungrateful. Didn't this pack of pusses realize that they had only been trying to help them? That all they had wanted to do was learn more about the wild cats of Piran.

There couldn't be any harm in that, surely?

Later, at rat headquarters, which was a dumpster hidden in a thicket of trees in the suburb known as Arze, General Rat paced up and down in front of his troops. "You are a miserable mischief of mice, the whole lot of you!" (In case you didn't know, a "mischief" is a group of mice, just as you might say a "flock" of sheep, or indeed a "rabble" of rats or "colony" of feral cats.)

"I give the order to hold your ground, and what do you do?"

"Uh, we, uh, swim away, sir?" replied one of the sergeant rats, reveling in his newfound eloquence.

"It was a *rhetorical* question."

"Huh?"

"Meaning to say, you gibbering idiot, that you weren't required to supply an answer!"

"Oh."

"I'm tempted to make an example of you, but we've lost enough lives today. They were *Yfrtbm* (Heroes)! And they shall be remembered as Yfrtbm, at least until they are forgotten!"

"Yfrtbm! Yfrtbm!!" chanted the rats, but to tell the truth, they were already beginning to forget the rats that had died that day. They hadn't exactly been very popular rats. Mind you, what rat ever is? Aside from General Rat. And the only reason he was the most "popular" rat was that he was the loudest and, in a pinch, the most ferocious.

Growing weary of so much sticky sentiment, General Rat motioned to two of his most trusted corporals to join him in private, at the bottom of the compost heap.

"If we made any mistake today, it was this: we tried to bite off more than we could chew."

"General?"

"I mean, the next time we attack, we make sure not only is there nowhere they can run, but we do it where we can go about our work unobserved."

"Ah, a stroke of genius, General."

"Of course it is! What do you expect from your brilliant leader?"

We shall not eavesdrop further on their conversation, most sensitive reader, for once again it is simply too revolting to audit. But to summarize, as humiliated and defeated as they felt, the rats of Piran would indeed be sure to fight another day. The wild cats of Piran would thus have to remain on the alert for this old enemy, one that had so obviously gained in strength and in cunning.

AND WHAT OF ZACH AND NIKI, THE YOUNG HUMAN COUPLE? How did they feel about their intervention in cat-rat affairs? Did they even *believe* what they thought they saw? Maybe they had sunstroke or perhaps they had drunk too much wine at dinner the night before. That would not have been so unusual for Zach, but Niki was of a somewhat steadier disposition.

The adult human mind is very quick to find so-called rational explanations for such things. As Zach and Niki walked back to their hotel in silence, they were both already rewriting what they'd seen. "It all happened in a flash, didn't it?" Zach said eventually.

"It's hard to tell."

"Yes, I suppose that's what I feel as well. . . ."

"We've both been under an enormous amount of stress recently," said Niki, and Zach could only concur.

The human mind isn't particularly supple when it comes to such matters—at least, not compared to the psyche of untamed Piranese cats. But the following night they both lay awake in the dark, repeatedly piecing together what they had seen, then imagining it from different perspectives. It was as if they were directing a film, a film about cats that were highly animated.

When Zach suggested prolonging their stay in Piran another night or two, Niki acted as if doing so was the most natural thing in the world. This was unusual because they both had something they called "careers" back in London.

In the crypt, Felicia and Dragan were treated as heroes by the other wild cats. Especially after the two of them had described in detail how heroic they had been. It's enough to say that all of the cats were mightily relieved that their best and brightest were alive to fight another day. At the same time, although the wild cats had done a good job of depleting rat numbers, they were quite sure they'd be hearing more from them. And what about that young human couple? What could anyone say about that? The two lucky cats discussed the battle from their own perspectives, stressing their own bravery and downplaying the human role, which is the wild cat way.

As Dragan said: "It's been a big day." And as Magyar said, "Day big a been it's." The entire colony of the wild cats of Piran was now well aware that the peninsula's rat population had become the team to beat this season, and that it had a leader, one capable of strategic thought.

Of course there had been one more surprise for the other wild cats that morning. Leopold had been waiting outside the entrance of the crypt for a signal from Felicia.

"Come in, Leopold. You're among friends here," she said finally. The mere mention of his name caused the fur on the back of Magyar's neck to stand up. You can forget anything you've heard about Austro-Hungarian alliances. This particular Hungarian tabby cat bore his fellow feline from Vienna little affection.

"Leopold . . . has decided he cannot live without us," Felicia declared as Leopold made his entrance. He blushed at this remark, the white of his tuxedo coat turning pink with embarrassment.

"Use good to him put better!" grunted Magyar.

"Don't worry, my Hungarian friend," said Leo-pold. "To good use I shall indeed be put—my first task being to draw up a plan to rescue Beyza from the house which, I believe, you call Dogboy Villa."

That silenced Magyar for a while, which was an achievement in and of itself. But what indeed of that grander plan, to rescue Beyza from captivity? After pausing to gather your breath if necessary, do read on to find out.

8

Like Herding Cats

It is said the best-laid plans of mice and men often go askew, but what of the plans made by crafty cats from Austria? The answer lies in the ensuing pages.

It was early in the evening at Dogboy Villa, and little Beyza the cat was biding her time until darkness, until night set in, which is when she planned to make her first tentative attempt to escape from the humans and dog who held her captive. She had been put in an unused room in the villa. Here the childhood toys and mementoes of both Fisko and his sister Ivana were gathering dust.

For Ivana, childhood toys meant dolls and their clothes and houses, as well as a goodly number of books. She had been particularly fond of a series about an eleven-year-old girl detective who solved mysteries no adult could ever fathom. Yes, Ivana was a kindly, intelligent sort; all the evidence pointed to that. Once she grew out of music that made Beyza's head hurt, talking endlessly on the telephone, and drenching herself in makeup and perfume, she would be quite an acceptable sort of human girl.

As for Fisko, well, that was a different matter altogether. All of his toys had to do with war, crime, and violence in general. Guns and knives and still more guns, and an awful lot of computer games with names like "Complete Destruction IV" and "Assault and Battery XII." They were games in which a skillful player could wipe out an entire civilization in the space of an afternoon. A certain amount of this was normal in a lot of children, especially boys, but in Fisko this interest had been taken to its extreme.

Beyza had the acute sense of hearing so typical of cats, and there were sounds coming to her from within the house. She pressed her delicate pink ear up against the bedroom door and listened. It was Fisko and Ivana, and it sounded very much as if they were going to leave the house *together*. This was something that hadn't happened before. Indeed, from what Beyza had observed, the teenage brother and sister did almost everything possible to stay out of each other's way. When they were in the same room for more than a minute or two, some argument always erupted.

"You told me I could give that stupid cat to Katya as a present," the boy was yelling. "That is the only reason it is even alive!"

"I didn't say anything of the kind. I will look after her."

"Oh yes, and what about when Mama and Papa get back? The kindest thing would be to put it out of its misery now." This didn't sound good at all to Beyza.

"We can give her to Katya before Mama and Papa come back." Ivana didn't sound too sure about this, and in fact it sounded like she was playing for time— Beyza's time.

"C'mon, Fisko, d'you want to meet with Katya or not?"

Beyza couldn't exactly understand the response, but she assumed he'd said yes. Soon there were more teenager-getting-ready sounds: the radio playing, a hair dryer blowing, doors and cupboards opening and closing loudly. The voices grew close again, and louder, joined by the sound of footsteps in the hallway. Last but not least came the noises of a panting dog: the boy's fearsome-looking German Shepherd.

"Oh, no, no, no. You're not bringing Thor with you," the girl said. "We're going to meet at a nice café in Portorose, and then maybe, if Katya doesn't completely hate you by that point, we'll go to a discotheque. Leave the dog here."

"Ivana, you know I don't like taking orders from you or anyone."

"Fisko, do you want to be forced to go home because they won't let you inside the disco with a dog?"

Clearly, the boy Fisko was not one to listen to others, but his sister was occasionally able to appeal to what little sense he had.

"Oh, all right," he grumbled, in a triumph for rational deduction.

Beyza heard the boy go to the back door and let the canine out. Then she heard the footsteps drawing closer again. So she ran away from the door, to the little corner of the room that Ivana had made up for her—complete with scratch mat and kitty litter. The door opened and it was her, Ivana, kindly and affectionate girl that she was, checking in on Beyza, giving her one last cuddle before she went out. Fisko loomed in the doorway, sneering.

Eventually Ivana closed the door behind her and left the little Angora alone in the house, or so she thought.

Outside the villa was a desperate band of wild cats, ready for anything. Now that the sun had gone down it was time to implement the "covert mission" Felicia and Leopold had been planning. The wild cats had watched as the teenage brother and sister emerged from Dogboy Villa, locked the front door behind them, and disappeared down the hill on their way into the old town.

"Excellent, they are both out of the way for a while," said Felicia.

"And the dog is out back," agreed Leopold.

Now was no time to be a scaredy-cat. The cats advanced stealthily and with purpose upon the house, with Felicia at their lead, Dragan and Leopold not far behind.

INSIDE, BEYZA SENSED SOMETHING ON THE OTHER SIDE of the door that turned her innards to jelly: the unmistakable presence of dog breath.

With no further preliminaries, Thor, that great beast of a German Shepherd, came tumbling into the room, practically landing on top of her. Beyza squirmed and shrieked under the weight of such a creature. All she could think of in that moment was the noble Magyar, and how she was sure he would have sprung to her defense in a situation like this. He was such a brave and strong old Hungarian tabby tom, she thought to herself. This was ironic, because just a few days before, she had been referring to him as a "silly old puss." Interesting how absence can make the heart grow fonder. Absence, and a great big German Shepherd breathing down your neck.

OUTSIDE, THE CATS HAD SNEAKED UNDER A FENCE and crossed into what Felicia and Leopold referred to as "enemy territory." Leopold had studied the place carefully and discovered a small window the humans always left open when they left the villa—namely, the window of the downstairs lavatory. But that was a matter of small import. What was important was that there was a drainpipe right next to it, and that the wild cats of Piran could form a feline chain. The fattest of all the cats took his place, not without complaint; then Dragan climbed on top of him, as he was the second heaviest. Next came Magyar, himself generously proportioned. Felicia, leading from the front as always, scaled the pile of cats until she was high enough to leap through the open window. The other cats followed until the only three remaining cats were the fat cat, Dragan, and Magyar. Dragan gave a mighty heave, sending Magyar hurtling toward the window, where Leopold, now inside and on top of another pile, grabbed him by the front paws. Dragan grabbed hold of Magyar's hind legs, and the fat cat grabbed hold of his. And so they went. One on top of another, whoops-a-daisy, let's make sure we don't all go falling down on top of each other now. Thus, one by one, they were soon all inside Dogboy Villa.

"Does it smell to *you* as if a dog has been in here recently?" Felicia asked everyone as they got back up on their feet inside the WC. On further examination, it appeared the door of this lavatory was locked from the other side: a source of much consternation among the cats, all wedged tight inside the functional little space.

"And how are we supposed to open this door from the inside?" Magyar demanded. "That you have thought about, my Viennese *wunderkind*?"

"You forget, comrade, that I grew up in the home of a Viennese master locksmith. There will be no Majikat necessary for this lock, just pure technique." Leopold produced a silver toothpick that had fallen from a Piran tablecloth decades ago and been stored in the crypt along with other such oddments and souvenirs. He slid the toothpick between his teeth, stood up on Dragan's broad shoulders, and gingerly inserted the toothpick in the lock.

"One . . . two . . . three. Oh, I see. Well, we must try again." There was one big disappointed sigh from Magyar's quarter.

"C'mon, Magyar, give him a chance," growled Dragan.

"It might take me a couple of times to get it right, you know. Very well. One . . . two . . ."

IN THE RUMPUS ROOM, BEYZA'S EYES WERE CLOSED as tight as could be, and she had curled up into a little fluffy white ball. She was waiting for the terrible biting pain that she thought was coming any second. Surprisingly brave in her own way, Beyza thought to herself: "Oh come on, dog, get on with it. I've got another five cat lives left." But nothing happened. Oh, a big splash of doggy drool fell—splat—on her cheek, but she was expecting the crunch of two rows of sharp teeth. Instead, a low, husky, and surprisingly kind-sounding voice spoke to her.

"Open your eyes, little one. I'm not going to hurt you," it said. Beyza opened one eye and looked up at the huge canine head hovering over her.

"I beg your pardon?"

"I said, little one, that you're safe with me."

"You wouldn't tease a poor little Angora puss, would you?" Beyza asked plaintively, fluttering her eyelids.

"No, I wouldn't. D'you know, I get tired of barking and gnashing my teeth all the time, but it's what is expected of a German Shepherd, isn't it? How I wish I'd been born a Chihuahua. You know, that's kind of the dog equivalent of an Angora. Small, fluffy, and cuddly; no one expects a Chihuahua to rip the head off cats, or chase small dogs and boys around."

"No, well, quite," agreed Beyza, still a bit nervous about this great beast leering over her. Better that it was friendly than not, but still. Dogs were hardly known for their subtlety or their cunning, but this one might be the exception. Maybe it was toying with her—who was to say?

"But I heard that boy lock you in the garden out back."

"You mean you heard him *try* to lock me out back. He's as stupid as he is brutish, that lad, which sometimes works to my advantage." He really was quite well spoken, for a dog, Beyza thought, examining the German Shepherd more closely. What's more, when it wasn't barking and growling and biting, it was actually a kindly looking face, with its great, big liquid eyes.

"Don't worry. I know all the angles around here," he said with unmistakable pride.

"But where did you learn to speak Cat?"

"My previous owner, may he rest in peace, also kept a cat. We were quite friendly and so I picked up the rudiments. For the rest, I keep my ear to the ground. I've picked up a reasonable amount of Rat too."

"Euugh." Beyza shivered at the mere thought of the Rat language. "Still . . . I don't understand. Why are you helping me?" she asked.

"Oh, I don't know. For one thing, I'd do just about anything to make that vicious oaf Fisko unhappy."

"Why stay with him at all?"

"It's in my nature. I'm a loyal, domesticated animal."

"But you'd be betraying your master if you help me escape."

"Do you want to go back to your fellow felines or not?" asked Thor, wearying of this tautology. Beyza didn't need to think too hard about *that* one. What choice did she have but to trust the German Shepherd?

"C'mon, then, my little friend. You can sit up on my shoulders." The big dog sat down again on his hind legs, and the little cat climbed up on his back. When he rose up to his full height, Beyza rode him like a cowgirl on a horse. And so they set off, leaving the rumpus room behind, and stepping out into the great unknown of the future.

"*Ein, zwei, drei,*" said Leopold ("one, two, three" in Human German), trying to unlock the lavatory door. As if that was going to make any difference. . . . But then, the splendid thing is that it just might have, because this time when he manipulated the lock with the little silver toothpick . . . What do you know? It worked! There was an audible click as the handle turned, and the door opened into the room.

As you may have observed yourself, cats are quite capable of squeezing through the narrowest of entryways. To put it another way, they can get *in* just about anywhere (especially as they are always elegantly dressed).

Imagine the sight of them now: This band of feral cats in the villa's hallway. They moved as stealthily as they could, even the fat cat, cocking their ears and sniffing the air to orient themselves to their surroundings. There was a very clear and distinct scent, but it was of dog, not boy. The cats followed their noses through the house, out the front door, and down to the long, winding driveway.

And there in front of them was Thor the German Shepherd, ambling down the path with Beyza on his back. On catching sight of the big German Shepherd the cats froze in their tracks, hissed, and stood up on their hind legs. Thor came to a halt as well, cocked an eyebrow, and regarded them with curiosity. The wild cats stood facing the dog with its prisoner across the mutual divide of language, culture, and species. Then they began hissing in unison, ready to attack. Thor couldn't help himself. He too now began to growl and gnash his teeth. Granted, while he might have been a pacifist in principle, principles were one thing, but instinct and a pack of feral cats hissing at him were another.

*Beyza the Turkish Angora riding on top of
Thor the German Shepherd's back.*

A tiny, impossibly cute voice was trying to be heard above all the noise. It was, of course, Beyza. "Please, cats, stop! Fellow felines, puh-leeze! Felicia, listen!"

But this was to no avail. It's hard to say what the precise signal was, because there didn't really seem to be one, except that as one conjoined body, the wild cats attacked Thor, jumping on his torso, clawing, scratching, and biting.

"Listen to me! He's my friend! He's trying to help me!" Beyza squealed.

"Oh Beyza, tish-tosh, *I'm* your friend!" Magyar said joyously, not listening to her either. In a rather swashbuckling sort of a move, he leapt up and grabbed Beyza in his big orange paws, carrying her to "safety."

The big German Shepherd was meanwhile struggling to fend off the wild cats. Of course individually he could have beaten any of them. But all the feral cats attacking simultaneously, now that was a different matter. He'd lost the end of one of his ears already, thanks to Dragan, who'd bitten it off and promptly swallowed it. Thor felt like he was going to black out because of the pain. He had begun to sink to the ground and the sky was spinning. If this kept up, it would soon be lights out for the German Shepherd, who, it had turned out, wasn't such a bad fellow after all.

"Magyar, if you don't save him, you will never be my friend, my special friend, again," said Beyza, grabbing the Hungarian tabby cat by the scruff of the neck.

Magyar didn't need to be told *that* twice over.

"IN THE CAT OF NAMES WHO ON THE MOON LIVE! CAAAAAAAATS! OUT IT CUT! (In the name of cats who live on the moon, cut it out, cats!)" Magyar shouted at the top of his old Hungarian windpipes. This had the desired effect right away. The cat-scratching and cat-clawing and cat-biting all stopped instantaneously. It turned out that the only thing supporting Thor had been all the cats holding onto him, and so the big dog now flopped unceremoniously to the ground. He lay there, still conscious, with one eye open.

"In the name of cats who live on the moon? What are you trying to tell us, Magyar?" Felicia was the first to ask. "In the name of 'lunar felines,'" Magyar replied, which more or less meant in the name of everything the wild cats held sacred. What had come over the Hungarian tabby cat, coming to the defense of a German Shepherd dog?

The Merchant of Venice

In which the reunion of those two starstruck lovers, Magyar and Beyza, finds unexpected symmetry on another plane.

By now, dear reader, you will have formed the notion that the moon is very important to the wild cats of Piran: the moon and its cycles, from new moon to full and back again. Surely too, you have noticed the shadows on the surface of the moon form the shape of a cat's face? If you can't see the resemblance straightaway, well then, tilt your head to one side slightly and squint. You see? There, the two eyes, the little snout nose, and the jowls of a cat? So it's hardly surprising the moon is important to cats, now is it?

So when Magyar cried out to the other cats, telling them to stop attacking Thor the German Shepherd—and did so in the name of cats who live in the moon—it had an instant effect.

"What are you trying to tell us, Magyar?" Felicia had asked, a little out of breath. But it was Beyza who answered.

"This fine German Shepherd's name is Thor, and really, his bark is much worse than his bite."

"Thank you, Beyza. You do me too much kindness," said the wounded and exhausted dog, and every cat there took a step back at the sound of a dog speaking in their own tongue.

"If you are such a friend to cats, then why do you bark and chase us so whenever we see you?" This was Felicia speaking now.

"You have seen who my master is, I take it? Beyza is correct, though. I bark a lot more than I bite. Indeed, I do as little damage as I can, and I help smaller animals as and when I can. Now don't be alarmed, you cats, but I'm going to get up now."

All the cats noted, just as Beyza had, what a kind-sounding voice the German Shepherd had. It may be that their sensitivity will one day be their undoing, but the wild cats of Piran all of a sudden felt very sorry for the bitten and battered dog that struggled to its feet in front of them. They really are very kind and decent cats. That is, unless you happen to be a rat, mouse, insect, or fish. Or you happen to get on their wrong side. Other than that, they're great.

"It's alright, Thor, is it? I will assist." This was Leopold, in diplomat mode.

"So will I," joined in Beyza.

"Mean you to say a dog has taken my place?" grumbled Magyar. Felicia ignored the ridiculous exchange that followed, with all its obvious jealousy and separation anxiety. Instead, as usual, she concentrated on what must be done next. "Come on," she eventually said. "Let's all get out of here. You might as well come with us. . . . Thor?"

"But . . . But . . . But how would we live, where would I sleep?" the German Shepherd asked.

"Never mind any of that. Just get out of here now—and come with us!"

"Oh, alright."

"Dogs," thought Felicia. "They're so easily led."

She was in for another surprise, though. Just as they reached the front gate, Thor changed his mind for a final time.

"Wait," he said, "I must stay. It's all become clear to me. I am much better off to you inside the villa, where I can keep an eye on the boy." Felicia, considering this, saw the sense in it at once.

"Tell me where your hideout is, and I will come visit you when I have information. Besides, if I go with you now, Fisko might trace my scent to your hideout. He is half-animal, that boy, but not in a good way. More like a lycanthrope, or werewolf. Really it is better I stay here."

Felicia decided she would trust Thor. So she told him the location of their hideout, the crypt in the Basilica of Saint George, before herding all the other cats away from the villa and on their way to safety.

After the boy Fisko had returned to Dogboy Villa, there had been a lot of screaming and shouting and throwing of things audible from within, but eventually that had settled down.

From thereon in, it was an evening on which anything other than celebration would have been out of order. So, in the stillness before dawn, Magyar and Beyza went skipping on all fours across Piazza Tartini, much as they had done just three nights before—when she, of course, had been captured. But on this night their hearts were filled with joy at the prospect of playing together again. Seeing what time it was by glancing at the moon's position in the night sky, Magyar suddenly remembered something.

"My darling Beyza," puffed Magyar as he drew to a halt on the piazza, "there's something you should see . . . but quiet be we must. . . ."

Beyza was about to tell him *she* would decide when to be quiet, when she saw what he was pointing at. Just as the very first hint of morning light tinged the clouds in the night sky, there was movement, or what looked like movement, on the balcony of the Venetian Merchant's House. It was the ghost of a young maiden, the same one as had appeared the other night. Beyza was as swiftly entranced by her as Magyar the tabby had been, the first time he laid eyes on this beauteous lass.

She did the same thing as before, this maiden, this comely young lady from another century. She stretched her hands out imploringly, her eyes shining with tears, her face a picture of unfulfilled longing. Then, as before, a smile began to play on her lips, and her face began to literally light up with delight.

Magyar, seeing the flicker of a smile and expecting the young maiden to vanish any second, rushed to comfort Beyza. For she, too, would no doubt experience the same feeling of emptiness as had he following the maiden's disappearance.

But then a strange thing happened. Instead of vanishing, the girl stayed on the balcony, which was flooded with light, like rays of sun peering through the clouds after a storm. The smile on the ghost lady's face grew even wider, as if she was so happy that she was only just managing not to laugh out loud. Then she began waving at something in the middle distance, something that seemed to be coming from the direction of the Adriatic Sea. The same thought occurred to both Magyar and Beyza. They both turned their heads at the same time toward the source of the light, toward the sea. What they saw, no feral cat of Piran—and certainly no human being—could have possibly seen in centuries.

Out on the sea, sailing toward the market square of Piran, was a fifteenth-century Venetian sailing ship. It was a single-masted, square-rigged merchant ship, flat-bottomed with a straight keel and a shallow draft. Its mainsail blew in an imaginary wind, and more than twenty-five pairs of oars rowed by sailors stripped to the waist helped propel her closer and closer to the shoreline. Fluttering above the mast were flags or, rather, pennants decorated with the Venetian colors. And can you guess, or do you perhaps already know, dear, inquisitive reader, what the Venetian flag looks like? Well, above a burgundy red background, and weaved in a golden thread, is a picture of a lion, with wings. *"The winged lion that grasps territories, seas, and stars."* The lion of Venice! To so many humans it was merely a symbol of the past, but to the wild cats of Piran, it represented everything they'd once been and could be again one day.

It is important to mention, of course, that this was indeed a *ghost* ship, a phantom vessel, so although it sailed as if plowing through the sea, the water was untouched by its presence. Indeed it created not a single ripple on the waves. Magyar and Beyza watched, awestruck, and the Venetian galley ghost ship glided over the embankment on the piazza and drew up outside the Venetian Merchant's House.

An imposing figure stood on the poop deck of the galley, his hands at his side and his legs apart. He had a trim beard, was dressed in a velvet cap and heavy fur coat, and his gloves were encrusted with jewels. Indeed he was the very image of a wealthy, fifteenth-century Renaissance gentleman. Neither Magyar nor Beyza would have described him as handsome, perhaps, but he was a striking sort of figure. Certainly, the beauteous woman standing on the balcony must have thought so. For after blowing him a kiss, in a most dainty fashion, she ran inside, only to reappear a few minutes later at the front door of the rose pink fifteenth-century house.

The ghost ship hovered above the piazza, having sailed as close to port as it would have done in the fifteenth century (before the inner harbor was filled in and replaced with Piazza Tartini). The door of the Venetian Merchant's House opened, and the golden-haired maiden ran toward an invisible waterline. This was where the old fifteenth-century wharf had ended. A plank shot down from the side of the ship, and this merchant of Venice (for surely he could be no other) walked briskly down it, barely able to contain his excitement as he hurried to her side.

They embraced, and as they did, three trumpet-ers stood up on the deck of the boat, which, inciden-tally, was called the *Venus*. A fanfare blasted forth from their flag-draped horns.

Then, the sound of a violin drifted down from Tartini House. It must have been the old violinist Giuseppe Tartini himself or, rather, his ghost. No one else either living or dead could play as beautifully as that. A heavenly choir and invisible orchestra joined in with the glorious noise coming from Tartini's win-dow. Down on the piazza Magyar took Beyza by the paw, sweeping her off her hind feet.

As they danced, a shooting star sped across the night sky. The merchant of Venice and the maiden of Piran stood on the deck of the Venetian galley, which then sailed away into the horizon of the dawn's early light.

*The Venetian galley ghost ship
sails into the harbor of Piran.*

It was as if the night sky and the ghost world had joined in league with Magyar and Beyza's happiness.

MAGYAR AND BEYZA'S REUNION WAS, you might say, always meant to be. Whatever the faults of these two, their affection for each other was genuine, and had been ever since they had first met. That was years ago, and hundreds of miles away, on the Hungarian puszta. When he met her, Beyza was struggling to survive, having been mislaid by her owner, a very wealthy and silly woman who thought of her cat in the same terms she might have thought about a new handbag.

"Accidentally abandoned" and now pelted by the puszta's late-winter winds and rain, the little Angora was getting rather desperate when he, Magyar, had shown up. He taught her the ways of the wild: how to be self-reliant and not depend on humans for home comforts—all the tricks of their trade. Progress had been slow at first, but eventually Beyza caught on. As we have seen, in her own way, she was now quite a tough customer.

Not content with the Hungarian countryside, she had longed to visit the great capitals of the earth, and to see its wonders. So, together they had headed south, eventually jumping a train that took them all the way to the Turkish city of Istanbul. Here, in the ancient city, they had dined every night on sweetbreads and sultanas. That part of the trip had been all right, as far as Magyar was concerned. In fact, he could have settled happily in the old port city, but Beyza had scarcely begun her wanderings. Yet it was as if something, all along, had been pulling them toward Piran.

A change was now wrought in Magyar with the rescue of Beyza; for finally he realized that Piran had become his home, and he longed for no other. He belonged with Beyza, and they belonged here, in this enchanting, and enchanted, place.

FELICIA, DRAGAN, AND LEOPOLD HAD WATCHED the ghost ship from a discreet distance.

"Do you hear that violin?" asked Leopold. "That's Tartini."

"He can certainly scratch out a tune," said Dragan, in his rough way.

"Come and meet him properly some time," said Leopold, looking directly at Felicia.

"I'll think about it," she replied, looking directly back at him.

"I heard he was in league with the Devil," Dragan said. "Or *a* devil, anyway. That's why I always stayed away from his house."

"*Anche io* (me too)," said Felicia, much to Leopold's chagrin. But then: "My, listen to that. He does play beautifully—too beautifully to be all bad. So, perhaps one night you will take us to him, Leopold."

"I'm coming, too," said Dragan, "whether you like it or not."

"Of course, Dragan," Leopold replied, "but I didn't know you cared for music." He would have much rather just gone alone with Felicia, as Dragan must surely have known.

"It's not up there with eating fish, I'll give you that. But I do like a nice tune." In fact, what Dragan liked more than anything was to see Felicia happy and taken care of. If Leopold's return to the colony made her happy, that was fine with him. But he wasn't sure what to make of this Tartini business. After all, the old legends really did say Tartini had taught the Devil how to play the violin. What were they getting themselves into?

This troubled Dragan, but at the same time he could see there was much to celebrate. They had survived a rat onslaught and rescued Beyza. The feral felines of Piran had also gained an important new ally in the battle against rats. This, of course, was the German Shepherd Thor.

"So, Thor is not *man's* best friend, then?" Dragan later remarked, just as they were all drifting off to sleep in the crypt.

"S'pose not. Might be our new best friend, though," said Felicia. And, later: "He's right, though, this Thor. There is something very wolfish about that boy."

"Maybe he really is a wolfman?" suggested Dragan, only half seriously.

In any event, eventually Thor got into the habit of sneaking out of his kennel and out the back of his villa to join the wild cats of Piran in the crypt that was their crib. He often had useful information. He would tell them about the rat that he had caught and eaten that day. Just as usefully, he'd let them know if the lad Fisko was going to be away for a night—or on the warpath again.

At first, some of the wild cats of Piran felt a bit apprehensive about a dog calling on them most evenings. After a fairly short while, however, Thor's forthright but gentle manner won them over, and Thor was universally well-liked. "Who'd have thought? My best friends, a pack of feral cats," Thor would laugh to himself occasionally.

But let's not get ahead of ourselves. Well, no more than we already have. For while it can be safely said the wild cats had won their last round of battles, they were a long way from winning the war.

That, as they say, is another story; indeed, another entire *book* full of stories. But, gentle, sweet, kind, and intelligent reader, for now all you need to know is that, while they still lived in a constant state of danger, this whole colony of cats remained as composed and as nonchalant as ever. Felicia, Dragan, Leopold, Magyar, Beyza, and all the others still comprised the most impressive feral feline fighting force on the Adriatic, a reputation they intended to maintain. There may have been arrivals and departures in Piran, but the wild cats of Piran endured, somewhere in the deep of night, playing in the shadows and the moonlight.

Now wouldn't it be a shame if it were any other way?

POSTSCRIPT

Surely that cannot be "it," you cry, for the wild cats of Piran and their adventures? After all, if that was Chronicle *One*, surely its very name hints at the existence of a Chronicle Two? We haven't properly met Tartini, the violin-playing ghost, and who can say whether the boy Fisko will be on the warpath again!? Surely there will be more trouble from General Rat and his rodent army? The General doesn't seem the type to give up easily. And what about the storyteller, whose presence may be felt in these pages? Will he ever be so kind as to reveal his true self? Well, all good things come to those who wait. *The Wild Cats of Piran: Chronicle Two* will be available before all too long. And what a relief that will be!

ALSO AVAILABLE FROM
YOUNG EUROPE BOOKS

978-0-9850623-8-5

"A breathless . . . adventure. . . .
Meticulously imagined."
—*Kirkus Reviews*

"Ellis's . . . years living in
Eastern Europe give this
steampunk fantasy . . . a
strong sense of place and an
unerring ear for the newspeak
of totalitarianism."
—*Publishers Weekly*

"The blend of magic
and machinery is eerily
intriguing."
—*Bulletin of the Center for
Children's Books*

Young Europe Books

Young Europe Books,
an imprint of New Europe Books,
presents a new face of the Old World
abounding in youthful energy, emotions, and fantasy.

ABOUT THE AUTHOR

Scott Alexander Young can't quite decide if he's a dilettante or a Renaissance man. A TV scriptwriter, writer, and actor from New Zealand who lives in Budapest, Hungary, he is the creator and writer of *Max's Midnight Movies*, a TV series about cult cinema. As a character actor, he's popped up in television miniseries including *Dracula, Fleming,* and *Houdini.* In his side career as a travel writer, Young has been everywhere from Alaska to Buenos Aires, Hawaii to Florence—not to mention Piran, which he visits at least once a year.

ABOUT THE ILLUSTRATOR

From his studio in Trento, northern Italy, the Swiss/Italian artist **Moreno Chistè** has produced thousands of lively and colorful illustrations for companies such as Disney, Warner Bros., and Mattel. His work ranges from comics to advertising artwork, storyboards, merchandising, and entire collections of greeting cards for the major European card companies.